Praise for Shann

MW01241194

5 Cups! "*Shannon Stacey writes a story with a good solid plot and entertains with friction between the characters that leaves the reader mesmerized...It is a story of letting go and learning to love again. Ms. Stacey gives her characters strength and also shows them human...I give it a 5-cup rating.*" ~ Cherokee, Coffee Time Romance

"*A character-driven story of family and love, FOREVER AGAIN is definitely a winner.*" ~ Jennifer Bishop, Romance Reviews Today

"*Forever Again captured me from the first chapter and held me to the last...In my opinion Shannon Stacey knocked it out of the park with Forever Again! When a story sucks me in so deeply that I get involved as though it were happening to me, the author has done their job in writing an excellent story...Get Forever Again today. You'll laugh, you'll cry, you'll yell, and at the end you'll be satisfied!*" ~ Dee Valentine, Joyfully Reviewed

FOREVER AGAIN

By Shannon Stacey

A Samhain Publishing, Ltd. publication

Forever Again
Copyright © 2006 by Shannon Stacey
Cover by Scott Carpenter
ISBN: 1-59998-044-4
ISBN: 1-59998-001-0
www.samhainpublishing.com

Samhain Publishing, Ltd.
PO Box 2206
Stow OH 44224

First Samhain Publishing, Ltd. electronic publication: January 2006
First Samhain Publishing, Ltd. print publication: April 2006

FOREVER AGAIN

By Shannon Stacey

Dedication

For Stuart, who is the most amazing, dedicated and loving father to our children; and for Angela, whose judgment and eye for the story are a writer's best friend.

Chapter One

Gena heard the crunch of tires on gravel and her gaze flew to the mantel clock. She wasn't expecting anybody else—it had to be them. *Oh my God, they're early.*

After dropping the basket of fresh fruit next to the pastries on the sideboard, she reached up to pat the braid restraining her unruly mass of auburn hair. It would have to do because there was no time to brush it out now.

On her way to the front door, she straightened the vase of lilac boughs and laid a pen across the open guest registry book. Butterflies tickled her stomach as she thought about how much this weekend meant to her and her daughter.

Kristen Sinclair, the top news anchor in Boston and something of a New England celebrity, was getting married and she was considering Gena's bed-and-breakfast for her reception and honeymoon. That not only meant a lot of money, but some good publicity for the Riverside Inn, as well. With Mia's growing collection of college catalogs staring her in the face, every little bit helped.

So she and her daughter had spent the last ten days living and breathing according to their lists. To-do lists, to-buy lists. To-clean lists. Everything was perfect for Sinclair—party of two.

By the time Gena stepped out onto the porch, Kristen Sinclair was standing in front of a silver Mercedes giving instructions to a person unseen behind the open trunk lid.

Gena recognized her immediately from television. She was tall, lithe, and had a flawlessly coiffed helmet of bottle-blonde hair. The clothes, which hung perfectly on her body, probably cost more than Gena's entire wardrobe. She ignored the quick pang of envy and smiled.

"Ms. Sinclair, welcome to the Riverside Inn," she said, as she walked to the car and extended her hand. "I'm Gena Taylor."

They heard a muttered curse and what sounded like a head banging against the bottom of the trunk lid.

Ms. Sinclair rolled her eyes in the direction of the car and shook Gena's hand. "It's nice to meet you. We left early to beat the traffic, and there really wasn't any. And if he ever gets his head out of the trunk, I'll introduce you to my fiancé, Travis Ryan."

"Travis Ryan?" Gena repeated as the earth seemed to shift beneath her feet. *It can't be him. It's just a coincidence.*

"He's from here originally," Kristen said over her shoulder, as she walked toward the house.

That was no coincidence. *It's really him. My ex-husband wants to have his reception at my bed-and-breakfast? And his honeymoon?*

Gena suddenly felt sick. She remembered feeling that way when she was staring at the pregnancy test, unable to believe it was positive. And then again during the nightmare of bitter, accusatory phone calls between their parents that had ended with a stunned boy and an emotionally wrecked girl standing in front of a Justice of the Peace, repeating vows they didn't mean in toneless voices. And she had felt that way again when he walked out on her, convinced she was lying.

He thought she had lied about having his baby. *So what am I going to do about Mia?*

CLEANSKEIN

Travis Ryan kept his head hidden in the trunk, taking deep, ragged breaths to combat his shock and anger.

Gena Taylor. He swore again while rubbing the top of his head. It had taken fifteen years to put her far enough behind him to consider marriage again, and now here he was—right on her doorstep. But there was no way in hell she was hosting his reception.

This entire trip had been a big mistake. He had told Kristen again and again he didn't want to get married in New Hampshire. They lived in Boston and their friends lived in Boston. Why not marry there and honeymoon in the Caribbean?

Because it's romantic, she'd said. Weddings should take place in the bride's hometown. She was a military brat and didn't have a place to call home, so his would have to do.

What she really meant was that it was a better story. More interesting, more newsworthy. She was one of the best at taking an everyday event and making it headline news. All she needed was the angle.

Well, she's got one now, he thought.

He'd convinced himself that Gena Taylor would be long gone, off to make her life somewhere else. She wouldn't stick around after what she'd done, not in this gossip haven of a town. But this was just his luck. Of all the inns in the state, Kristen had to find the one owned by his lying, scheming ex-wife.

She hardly even qualified as an ex-wife. They had only been married for thirteen days. Thirteen days that he had wandered through in a fog, shell-shocked. Gone were the dreams of playing football at Boston College. Gone were thoughts of frat parties, cheerleaders, and making the big bucks.

He'd been stuck with a girl he didn't really know—with a baby on the way—and he thought his life was over. Until he spotted the panties stained with blood in the laundry basket.

She had actually managed to trap him into marriage by faking a pregnancy.

Not for long. He had tossed the panties and his twenty dollar wedding band on the table in front of her and walked out the door. He didn't even pack his things. The divorce was handled by his parents' lawyer and he never saw her again.

Until now. The temptation to get back in his car and go home was strong. But how would he explain this to Kristen? She worked hard, and she had spent the last week looking forward to relaxing and having nothing to do but sit on the porch and think about their wedding. This would definitely ruin her weekend.

Fifteen years was a long time. *She might not even remember me,* he tried to convince himself. But that wasn't likely. A woman probably didn't forget the man whose life she almost destroyed.

Gena willed the violent trembling to stop and tried not to think about Mia. She was aware of Kristen admiring the porch of the two hundred-year-old farmhouse, with the handcrafted swing and the fragrant climbing roses, but her focus was entirely on the unseen man behind the car.

For the first few years of Mia's life she had been afraid he would find out about their baby. She thought he would come back and want to see his daughter—maybe even take her away. His parents had moved to Boston with him, but she thought they would stay in touch with old friends. She stayed close to home during her pregnancy, but there were a lot of people in town who knew that Mia was Travis's daughter. But as the years passed and she never heard from him, she started to relax.

Now he was back. But she wasn't a kid anymore. She could handle this. This was business. And it was business she couldn't turn away. There was no possible way the Sinclair-Ryan reception could be held at the Riverside Inn now, but Kristen could still enjoy a relaxing weekend at a B-&-B she might love enough to recommend to her friends.

If Travis just plays along. Gena was betting he hadn't told his fiancée about her. They wouldn't have gotten their license yet, so she might not even know she was becoming wife number two. And Gena wasn't about to tell her.

Hopefully Travis wouldn't either. She would welcome him and put the ball firmly in his court. He could either take his fiancée and get back in the car, or stay and make the best of it.

One foot in front of the other, she told herself as she moved around the Mercedes. *I can…*

The thought died the instant she laid eyes on Travis Ryan. For a second she was back in high school again and her stomach tightened just as it always had when she was brave enough to cast a glance in his direction.

Time had etched its passing on his face, but the character lines framing his eyes and mouth only added to his rugged charm. His still impossibly thick golden hair showed no signs of receding, and his eyes were exactly the same brilliant blue she saw every time she looked at Mia. The years had given him a chiseled, confident look that was almost devastating.

At that moment she was thankful for the trunk lid hiding them from Kristen's view. She didn't need a mirror to know that she looked pale and nervous. Far more nervous than having an important guest like Kristen Sinclair merited.

Gena had to clear her throat before she could speak. "Welcome to the Riverside Inn, Mr. Ryan."

He didn't say anything for what felt like an eternity, and she actually wondered if he was just going to ignore her.

It wouldn't be the first time Travis Ryan had simply pretended she didn't exist. He had done that from kindergarten right up until six weeks before they graduated. She had to admit her life had been a lot less complicated before that night.

"Don't ruin Kristen's weekend," he finally said in a voice that had deepened over the years.

Careful to keep her tone neutral, Gena said, "There's no reason for that to happen. I have minimal interaction with my guests as a rule."

"I hope you realize there's no way in hell I'm having my reception here now."

"I didn't think you would. And I don't really want to throw a party celebrating your second marriage anyway."

Travis leaned forward, his face a mask of tightly controlled anger. "Kristen might legally be my second wife, but she's the first woman I've ever *wanted* to marry."

That hurt. A lot. She hadn't forced him to marry her. That had been their parents' fault. Well, her parents mostly, but the wedding wouldn't have taken place if the Ryans hadn't thought it was the right thing to do. "I didn't want—"

"Travis? Ms. Taylor?" Gena could hear the crunch of Kristen's heels on the gravel. "Is there a problem?"

Gena didn't look away from Travis's stony gaze until he abruptly turned and began pulling designer suitcases out of the trunk. She turned and smiled convincingly—she hoped—at his fiancée. "No problem. I was just admiring your luggage, Ms. Sinclair."

The woman waved a dismissive hand at the expensive pieces. "Thank you. And please call me Kristen."

"Only if you'll call me Gena. Would you like some coffee and pastries before I show you around? I always set out a late afternoon snack for my guests."

"That sounds lovely. Not too much, though, or my personal trainer will shoot me."

A personal trainer? No doubt she had a personal shopper, too. Plus a personal assistant, and who knew what else? A personal masseuse, a personal back scrubber?

That would be Travis's job. The pang of jealousy she felt surprised Gena, and she didn't like the feeling.

She definitely needed to date more often. There was no way she would let herself lust after the man who had shattered her heart. Even if he wasn't her ex-husband, being the unknowing father of her child was an insurmountable complication. She had to grab the railing when she tripped on the porch steps. *Think about Mia later*, she told herself firmly.

Gena led them through the formal parlor where they deposited the luggage at the foot of the front stairs, and into the dining room. After brief introductions to the other guests, Gena excused herself. "Make yourselves at home, and feel free to look around. I have to see to...something, and then I can take you to your suite."

Without waiting for a reply, Gena walked into the kitchen, and through the door marked PRIVATE and into their personal living area. It had barely closed behind her before she leaned back against the wood.

This can't be happening. She pressed her hands to her face, trying to cool the searing heat in her cheeks. *How can I spend an entire weekend with him?*

Tears clouded her vision and Gena sank to the floor, resting her forehead on her knees. How many times had she cried in those days after she let him walk out? She could have made him stay, could have explained, but she let him go. She let him walk out the door, knowing she and her baby would probably never see him again.

But there he was, sitting in her dining room. The realization was like an avalanche, rumbling over her body and suffocating her with uncertainty. Seeing Travis with his fiancée made her feel that not-quite-good-enough feeling again—she was always second best. No doubt Kristen Sinclair had been a cheerleader, like the girl Travis had been dating in high school.

Gena had been in love with him since the day he let the classroom door swing shut on her that first day of kindergarten, awed by his good looks and his smile even then. The crush lasted through their elementary and middle school years, right into high school, but he had never seen her. She was frumpy, even pudgy at times, and always in pigtails. As they grew older there were pimples and bad haircuts— then the braces and her tendency to keep her nose in books. She grew accustomed to being invisible.

But he had noticed her once. Just once, and she had given herself to him without hesitation. He was a little bit drunk and she didn't ask him if he had a condom. She didn't want to spoil the moment she had been waiting for all her life. Six weeks later she took a pregnancy test.

They were only married for thirteen days when he walked out the door and she never saw him again. She had Mia, raised her with the help of her parents, and got her degree in small business management. It was another five years of constant hard work before she could get the loans she needed to open the Inn. But she had done it all—and done a good job—without a man in her life.

Sure, she'd dated. Over the years relationships had come and gone—some casual and one serious—almost to the altar. Working toward her professional goals and being a single mother had occupied most of her time. But she'd still had her heart broken a few times, and maybe broken one or two herself.

No, she wasn't the same person she'd been when Travis Ryan walked out on her. Now she was a mother, a businesswoman, and stronger than anybody had ever given her credit for. She could handle her ex-husband.

At least until their daughter got home. Mia was babysitting overnight for the Carter family and she wouldn't be home until at least noon tomorrow. That didn't give her much time, but she would have to think of some way to deal with the past exploding into their lives before then.

Travis toyed with a blueberry muffin, not really hungry, while Kristen explored the dining room and admired the assorted antique china. He tried to smile and nod in the right places, but his mind was somewhere else.

With his very much changed ex-wife to be exact. It was hard to believe she was the same Gena Taylor he was once married to. If he hadn't heard her name and her voice before seeing her, he never would have recognized her.

Taylor... Not Ryan and not something else. Why hadn't she remarried? In fifteen years she hadn't been able to find another unsuspecting fool to trick into marriage?

Or maybe she had. A lot of married woman kept their maiden names, or she could have reverted to it after a divorce. She obviously had the first time.

The years had been very kind to her—there was no doubt about that. Fifteen years ago she had been homely and shy, with no real future prospects. No doubt faking a pregnancy to catch herself a husband who *did* have prospects had seemed like a good idea at the time.

She'd have no trouble now. His ex-wife would turn any man's head. She had thinned out a little over the years, and while she wasn't nearly as lean as Kristen, her generous curves gave her a voluptuous appeal. Her simple white blouse and cotton twill pants suited her, showing off hips slightly widened by approaching middle age. Gone were the sloppy ponytails, replaced by a thick, glossy braid. Without the braces and teenaged acne, her face had matured into that of a beautiful woman.

Where Kristen was fussy and high-maintenance, Gena had a comfortable, natural air about her that appealed to him. He had never cared for the amount of makeup Kristen wore, and he noticed it more in contrast to Gena's clear, clean skin.

He wanted to see her hair loose, floating around her shoulders. He imagined slipping the elastic from the bottom of the braid and working his fingers through the woven tresses to free them. The hint of fire in her hair accented the flecks of gold in her hazel eyes, and…

Horrified by the direction his thoughts were taking, Travis forced himself to give his full attention to the hand painted creamer Kristen was holding under his nose.

"It's nice," he said, trying to sound sincere.

"I wonder where she found it."

"Probably at a yard sale," Travis said, instantly regretting the snide remark. If Kristen even suspected he disliked their hostess, she would demand an explanation. He simply wasn't ready to give her one. He wouldn't even know where to begin.

It certainly wasn't a time in his life he was extremely proud of. He had been dating Marcy Bishop for two years and she had never let him get beyond first base. He was frustrated and a little drunk when he saw Gena Taylor walking home from her job at the Dairy Queen.

He never could figure out what made him stop and offer her a ride. It was raining, but he'd passed her in the rain before and never cared. But that night he stopped and she climbed in. They hadn't gone very far down the road before he was mesmerized by the way her wet shirt clung to the very nice breasts he'd never noticed she had.

She'd been very willing when he pulled his truck behind the closed gas station and slid over to her side of the seat. He couldn't even remember now if he had kissed her, only that she'd had the funniest little smile on her face.

It was a warm and private smile. It seemed to speak of dreams coming true and contentment—even love. He remembered thinking at the time that she looked so happy, and he couldn't figure out why.

That smile had haunted him for weeks after. A few times he had almost called her, wanting to apologize for using her the way he had. But shame and guilt kept him from dialing the number he had looked up in the book.

His phone rang first. Gena's father told his father that she was pregnant and all hell broke loose. Not long after he was standing next to a girl he barely knew, promising to love and honor her til death did they part. He'd even pinched himself, standing there in front of the Justice of the Peace, but he hadn't awakened from the nightmare.

And that's why she had been smiling, he thought now. She was already scheming her way to the altar.

But he could survive one weekend with her. He probably wouldn't even see much of her. Then he'd tell Kristen the Riverside Inn wasn't exactly what he had in mind, and he would never see Gena again. She would be out of his life forever and he'd make damned sure he never came back to this town again—no matter how well she filled out her clothes.

❦❦❦❦❦

Gena exhaled deeply and walked back into the dining room. The other guests had taken some fruit and pastries and scattered to the porch or TV room, leaving Travis seated at the long harvest table while his fiancée examined the contents of the large glass-fronted hutch.

"I love your collection of china," Kristen said. "I'd love to collect things, too, but I don't have the time to dust."

Gena doubted very much that Kristen Sinclair did her own dusting, but she refrained from saying so. "Would you like to see the suite now?"

"Absolutely," Travis said quickly, giving her the impression that he was uncomfortable being in the presence of both women at the same time.

She led them to the addition she had put on a year after buying the Inn. It was on the ground floor, away from the private residence and the other guest rooms, offering honeymooners a sense of secluded privacy.

They walked into the small, charmingly country sitting room furnished with a sofa, chair, and two small tables. She showed them the TV and VCR hidden in one built-in cabinet, and the small refrigerator, microwave, and bar in another. Off to the left was the bathroom, large enough to accommodate the massive oval hot tub that sat in an alcove. This room had been the most costly improvement she made to the Inn, but it was a luxury that kept people coming back.

The bedroom was in the back. Gena had refinished the cherry king-sized sleigh bed herself, and her mother had made the exquisite double wedding ring quilt draped over it. The room was romantic without being overly feminine, and it had always been Gena's favorite.

Shannon Stacey

Seeing Travis standing in the middle of the hand-braided rug made her anxious to leave it, however. Especially when Kristen sat on the edge and dragged him down beside her.

"I just adore this room," she said, squeezing his hand.

Travis nodded, but didn't say anything. He was probably waiting for her to leave before he started pointing out reasons why they shouldn't hold their wedding reception here.

"Breakfast is served in the dining room from eight until ten in the morning, but I stop making omelets at nine-thirty. I always have pastries and beverages in the dining room from three to four in the afternoon."

She had promised Mia she wouldn't forget to mention the optional breakfast-in-bed service, but she didn't think she could handle seeing Travis and his fiancée tussled from sleep—maybe even lovemaking.

She had to struggle to keep her voice from shaking. "There's a basket of restaurant menus on the table in the sitting room, as well as a map of the town, which of course you don't need since…"

She broke off when Travis turned a startled glance her way. "Ms. Sinclair—Kristen, I mean—told me you were from here originally."

"He is," Kristen confirmed. "You guys look about the same age. Would you have gone to school together?"

"I didn't live here then," Gena lied, blurting out the first thing that came to mind. The tension went out of Travis's shoulders, and she cursed herself for covering for him. What did she care if he got in trouble with his fiancée? It would serve him right for not telling her the truth in the first place.

Kristen stood and slipped off her shoes. "The car ride up gave me a bit of a headache and I need some quiet time. Travis is so good with practical details, but I'm not in the mood to watch him count electrical outlets. Would you mind showing him around while I lie down for a bit?"

Would I mind? She'd rather walk across hot coals with a boa constrictor wrapped around her neck. "Of course I don't mind."

And she had her work cut out for her because Travis Ryan didn't look the least bit eager to be shown around.

ChApTeR Two

He looked even less amused once they were alone in the dining room again. "I'll find something to do on my own," he said in a tight voice. "You're the last person I need trying to *amuse* me."

Although it was hard, Gena managed to plaster a pleasant smile on her face. Hospitality was her business, and being rude was only going to make this situation worse.

"Would you like to see the grounds?" she asked as politely as she could.

He smirked and shook his head. "I can't believe you can talk to me like nothing ever happened. Not after what you did. I know it's been a long time, but you came *this* close to ruining my life."

Enough was enough. Politeness flew out the window in the face of his accusation. She pointed her finger at him, her spark of anger surprising them both. "Don't you think you've held that grudge long enough? I wasn't the only guilty party, Travis."

"*You* are the only one who pretended to be pregnant to catch a husband you didn't stand a snowball's chance of getting otherwise."

"I didn't..." Gena's words trailed off when she realized there was no way to deny his charges without admitting they shared a daughter. If she told him she really was pregnant when he left, she'd have to tell him about Mia.

So just tell him. The thought took her off guard, but she considered it for a moment. She could just look him in the eye and tell him he was a father. Maybe he did have a right to know, and he wasn't the only one clinging to an old grudge. She couldn't deny she was still angry about how he had treated her.

It looked like it was time to face the music. She only hoped Travis took the news better than he was taking seeing her again.

But she couldn't do it without talking to Mia first. Meeting her father face to face wasn't something Gena could just spring on her. For now she was forced to play the guilty party.

But a snowball's chance? That she didn't have to take. "Don't you think a little highly of yourself?" she asked in an edgy voice.

"Just being honest. You were too shy, and to tell you the truth, you weren't much to look at...then."

Their eyes met, and Gena felt heat creep up her neck and over her cheeks. So Travis Ryan thought she was attractive? Her heart skipped a beat even though it didn't matter. He was about fifteen years too late.

She bit down on an indignant reply and watched him pour another cup of coffee. If she was seriously going to consider introducing her daughter to this man, then she had to make peace with him. She wouldn't dump Mia in the middle of a conflict older than she was. Surely two mature adults could manage a little small talk.

"So tell me what you do for a living," she said in a softer voice as she sat across the table from him.

He looked at her warily, as if he suspected her of scheming to get at his bank accounts. "I counsel high school and college athletes."

Gena saw that having a discussion with him was going to be like pulling teeth. "Counsel them? Like a guidance counselor?"

"Not exactly. I'm in private practice. Kids that excel at sports feel a lot of pressure. The expectations are high, and when failure ceases to be an option for them, they start to crack. The pressure put on them by parents, coaches, teachers—even their peers—is extreme, and I help them cope."

"Did you feel that way? Is that why you do it?"

Travis leaned back in his chair and nodded. "I guess I did. After our…divorce, when I was back on track, the pressure was insane. Not only did I have the old expectations, but I had to redeem myself, too."

She almost apologized, but stopped herself. She had nothing to be sorry for. "What did you do?"

"I dropped out of B.C. in my sophomore year and took off—traveled around for a while. I needed to breathe—figure out who I was. Then I went back and enrolled in a community college and got my degree. I try to help kids before they reach that breaking point."

Gena smiled. "I never pictured you as the kind of guy who'd give up his dream to help others."

"I didn't give up on my dream. The dream just changed, that's all."

Gena felt unreal, sitting at her own table having a conversation with Travis Ryan. A civil conversation, no less. It was a good sign, and it gave her hope that he could be reasonable enough not to punish Mia for her mother's mistakes. *If I tell him.*

She couldn't remember every really talking to him. The night Mia was conceived the only thing she remembered him saying was, "Do you want a ride?" Their wedding night was spent apart—her on the couch crying, and him in the locked bedroom with the stereo turned up high. A few days later she had asked him if he'd thought of any names he might like for the baby and he'd left tread marks on the driveway in his rush to leave.

That's in the past, she tried to tell herself, but it was hard when the face of her adolescent dreams—and nightmares—was sitting across from her. How different would her life have been if she hadn't let him walk out the door without an explanation?

Travis swirled the last mouthful of coffee in the bottom of the cup because he couldn't think of anything else to do. It was awkward, sitting at the dining room table with a woman he'd done nothing but hate for fifteen years.

He tried to recall why she'd been so unpopular at school. He knew she was smart and a little bookwormish, but that wasn't such a bad thing. And she'd gone through a not-so-attractive stage, but she couldn't have been that bad if she came out looking like this.

He didn't know why he'd answered her questions either. It was none of her business what he did, and she'd lost her chance at cashing his paychecks. The Mercedes in the driveway was Kristen's, so if that's what made her so friendly, she was barking up the wrong tree.

Kristen. He had no idea how he was going to explain this to his fiancée. He'd always known that he'd have to provide proof of divorce to get their marriage license, and he'd planned to tell her about his first marriage before that happened. Just not yet.

Whenever he had considered telling Kristen about Gena, he had been too ashamed to find the words. While his ex-wife's crime was certainly greater, his own behavior had been almost as reprehensible. It wasn't something he was eager to share with the woman he was going to marry.

How would she react when she saw Gena Taylor's name on the divorce decree? He didn't want to tell her now and ruin her weekend, but when she found out later who their hostess was she would be livid. No doubt she would accuse him of hiding it from her—and lying to her—and he wouldn't be able to deny it.

He watched Gena stand and start piling dirty dishes onto a tray. She moved with a simple grace that lulled him into watching her work.

"I don't remember you being a redhead." He didn't mean to say it out loud.

She raised a hand to her hair and laughed, and the sound of it tickled the pit of his stomach. "It's not really that red, more of a brownish-auburn, but it has lightened as I've gotten older."

He refrained from telling her she looked good, and tried to keep his eyes on the table instead of her. He had little success. Her hips swayed ever so gently when she walked, and his gaze caressed the full roundness of her bottom.

"Damn," he whispered, getting Gena's full attention. He slammed the mug down and stood. "I'm going to watch TV in the suite until Kristen gets up. Then we'll grab some dinner. I probably won't see you again until breakfast."

Gena waited until after eight to put the sign on the kitchen door that announced she was out and listed her cell phone number. Her guests were either enjoying an evening out or in their rooms for the night, Travis and Kristen being among the latter.

She had stood at the window and watched the Mercedes leave, then heard them return two hours later. Kristen was hanging on his arm, laughing up at him, and Gena had turned away from the window when he smiled back at her. How many of her childhood years had she spent wishing he would smile at *her* that way?

Too many. All of them wasted, except for the moment they made Mia. And now it was time to try to explain that moment and all the decisions that came after it to her daughter.

During the short drive to the Carter house, Gena wrestled with her decision. Would telling Mia and Travis about each other do more harm than good?

She had the list in her pocket. Mia teased her constantly because she wrote out the pros and cons for almost every major decision she had to make. And she'd never made a decision bigger than this one.

Pros: Mia would have a father in her life. She didn't seem to miss having one and didn't often talk about it, but that didn't mean she didn't secretly yearn for one. And Travis would finally know Gena wasn't the scheming liar he thought she was. She'd been unpleasantly surprised to discover his opinion of her mattered enough to merit being on the list.

She hadn't seen the man in a decade and a half. He had trampled on her heart. Why should she care if he thought she was a lying gold-digger? But for some reason his words to her in the dining room had hurt, and she wanted him to know they weren't true.

A big consideration was the fact that she wouldn't have to go it alone anymore. She'd have a co-parent. She tried not to think about the college expenses lying in wait, but she couldn't help hoping Travis would contribute a little.

Cons: Mia would be angry when she found out her father had lived three hours away for her entire life. And what if she didn't forgive her for not telling Travis about her?

And what if Travis doesn't care? Maybe he and his wife-to-be didn't want a teenage daughter. If Gena told Mia about Travis only to be spurned by him, her daughter would be devastated.

The possibility of Mia not forgiving her alone was enough for the cons to outweigh the pros, yet she was doing it anyway. It was the right thing to do. She just hoped it wasn't a decision she would regret.

The Carter kids were young and should be in bed, so Gena knocked softly on the door.

"Who is it?"

"It's Mom," she said through the door.

"How do I know it's really you?" Mia asked, but Gena could hear the laughter in her voice.

"I know your middle name is Dawn."

"Public record."

"I know your lucky pair of underwear has Panda bears on the butt."

A little giggle. "So you're a perverted, drawer-snooping burglar."

"Who knows you have a crush on Mark Whittemore?"

"Mom!" Mia protested as she yanked open the door. "It's not a crush! It's unrequited love."

Unrequited love. Gena knew all about that. "We need to talk, sweetie."

Mia frowned and closed the door behind her mother. "What's wrong?"

"Let's sit down." Gena watched her daughter walk across the living room. She had her father's thick blonde curls, her father's Caribbean blue eyes. His height, his nose, his chin. It almost hurt just to look at her.

"Is it Gramma or Grampa?" Mia asked when they were settled on the sofa.

"They're fine, sweetie." She wasn't sure she could find the right words to tell her. "It's actually about…it's about Kristen Sinclair and her fiancé."

"Oh, no! Did they cancel?"

Gena shook her head, then took a deep breath. "Her fiance's name is Travis Ryan."

"Travis Ryan…My dad?" Gena nodded and Mia's eyes widened in surprise. "He's…She's marrying my father? He's at our house? Right now?"

"Yes."

Mia stood and started pacing, something she only did when she was very upset. "You said he left before I was born. He didn't know about me. How did he end up here?"

"It's just a coincidence. Kristen made all the arrangements and she had no reason to think we knew each other."

"He's the Travis Ryan who lives in Boston? The sports shrink?"

Gena was stunned, and her heart beat faster in her chest. "How did you know that?"

"Because I looked for him, Mom. On the Internet." She paced a faster, shorter line. "What did you expect? I don't have a dad. Kids are supposed to have dads. Of course I looked for mine."

How could I not know that? It was on the tip of Gena's tongue to ask if she had ever tried to contact him, but she already knew that answer. She would know if Travis had heard from his daughter.

"Why didn't you tell me you were trying to find him?" she whispered.

Mia stopped pacing to look at her. "Because I figured you would flip out. I didn't want you to think you're not good enough or anything."

But I'm not, am I? Her eyes brimmed with tears that spilled over onto her cheeks when she tried to blink them away.

"Did you tell him about me?" Mia demanded.

"I wanted to talk to you first."

"Great." Mia sat on the edge of the sofa.

She leaned toward her arm of the couch. Her arms were folded in front of her chest, and she crossed the leg closest to her mother over her other knee. Gena had no trouble reading her body language. *Keep your distance.*

"I called him once," Mia continued. "His secretary wouldn't let me talk to him unless I told her who I was, so I hung up. I thought I would know if he was the right guy if I heard his voice."

Pain squeezed Gena's heart like an iron fist. How could she not know Mia had been searching for her father? She was her mother, yet she hadn't even noticed the gaping hole in her daughter's life. Had she been telling herself Mia was fine for all this time just to avoid having to deal with it?

"So what now?" Mia demanded, hard-fought tears choking her voice. "What did Ms. Sinclair say when she found out you're his ex-wife? What did he say when he saw you?"

"He told me not to ruin her weekend. And she doesn't know. We…we pretended we don't know each other."

"What? How can you…." She stopped, shook her head. "Explain this to me again, Mom. You said he left before I was born because you guys didn't know you were pregnant and then he was gone. Is that all there is to it? If I'm going to meet him I want to know everything."

Gena looked at her daughter and sighed. The girl was pale and trembling, her body a livewire of emotion. She wanted desperately to pull her onto her lap and stroke her blonde curls like she used to, but she kept her hands folded in her lap. She felt vulnerable—fragile—and she didn't think she could take Mia pushing her away right now.

"Travis and I got married because I was pregnant with you."

"But you said-"

"Just let me tell it," Gena interrupted, a little more sharply than she'd intended.

She took a deep, calming breath. "We had sex one time, and I got pregnant. Our parents pressured us to get married. So we did.

"About two weeks later he found a pair of my panties in the laundry. I'd had some spotting, which the doctor said was okay if I took it easy, and I was too sick to rinse them out right then.

"But Travis found them and jumped to the conclusion that I was having my period, and that I faked the pregnancy to make him marry me. He threw the panties on the table and walked out. Today was the first day I've seen him since."

Mia rubbed her temples, digesting the information. "Why didn't you tell him he was wrong? Why did you just let him leave?"

"You can't even begin to imagine how unhappy we were, Mia. He hated me so much for ruining his dreams. College, sports scholarships, a big career. It was all gone because of me. I always thought being married to Travis Ryan would be a dream come true, but it wasn't. It was a nightmare. It was hell, Mia. And as tough as this situation is, you wouldn't be any better off being raised by two parents who were so miserable."

"How do you know?" The shock was wearing off and Mia's body shook with anger. "You could have gotten divorced and I could have lived with you and visited him on weekends and holidays like all the other kids do. He could have come to my school plays and my piano recitals. All the other kids..."

Her words trailed off and she broke into tears, great heaving sobs that wracked her thin body.

Gena pulled her daughter close and cried softly into her hair. "I'm so sorry, baby. I didn't know you hurt this much. I was just a kid and I did what I thought was right."

Mia jerked back, her tear-soaked face angry. "You haven't been a kid for a long time and you could have told me. You just didn't want to share, so I lost my dad."

"Sweetie, I—"

"I want you to go, Mom," Mia said, and Gena thought her heart would shatter like cold glass. "I'm going to call Denise to come over and stay with me. I'll call you tomorrow sometime."

"Mia—"

"Please, Mom. I just need to think about all of this, okay? You need to understand that."

"I love you, Mia. No matter what else you think, you need to know that's true. It's the truest thing in my life."

"I love you too. I just want to figure this out by myself. Before you tell him."

Travis sat deep in the shadows of the wraparound porch, his head back against the wicker rocker, a half-empty glass of scotch in his hand.

When he found the scotch in the honeymoon suite he had decided a stiff drink and some fresh air would do him good. After listening to

Kristen talk to her personal assistant on the telephone for almost an hour he realized she wouldn't even know he was gone. So much for her vow to spend the weekend doing nothing but enjoying the inn.

But here in the dark, where he thought he would dwell on his upcoming marriage, he found himself instead thinking about his ex-wife.

Gena Taylor, he mused silently. She was the last person he ever thought he'd sit at a dining room table and have a conversation with. Once he relaxed he had actually enjoyed her company for a few minutes.

And that disgusted him. She had almost ruined his life and there was no way he would forgive her for that just because he felt comfortable in her dining room—fifteen years later or not. That was her business, after all. As an innkeeper it was her job to make people feel at home—to feel like family. And deception was one thing she was very good at.

The soft purr of the minivan's engine broke into his thoughts. She was home. He had heard the van leave about an hour before, and he had hoped to be back in the suite before she got home so there would be no chance of bumping into her.

She didn't see him in the shadows, but when she stood under the light he saw that she had been crying. Was *still* crying, actually. Her head was bowed and her shoulders stooped, and for one crazy moment Travis felt an urge to comfort her.

Just a hug, he told himself, but he was too smart to let himself act on it. Holding Gena in his arms wasn't a good idea. He wasn't sure if it was because he had good reason to hate her, or because his traitorous body seemed to have forgotten that good reason, but he knew his relationship with his ex had to stay strictly hands-off.

Chapter Three

The next morning, he had to admit that she made one heck of a breakfast.

Kristen limited herself to a piece of fruit and a slice of dry toast while she chatted with two other guests. Travis feasted on blueberry pancakes with real New Hampshire maple syrup, eggs poached to perfection, and bacon fried to just the right degree of crispness.

While he ate he kept an eye on Gena. He hated to admit it—even if only to himself—but her appearance worried him. Her face was puffy and her eyelids were heavy, and it was obvious she had been up all night crying.

Travis knew it had something to do with wherever she'd gone last night, but he had no idea what it could be.

A lovers' quarrel, maybe? She didn't wear a ring, and there was no evidence of a man about the house. None of the guests had mentioned anybody else. If there was a husband or boyfriend around, he probably would have been seen by now.

Not that Travis cared. Gena's personal life was none of his business. He may have been married to her once, but he barely knew her. And he didn't want to get to know her any better.

Just keep telling yourself that, he thought angrily. The amount of time Gena spent in his thoughts was beginning to disturb him. He wanted to pretend she didn't even exist, but it wasn't working. It took every ounce of willpower he had to not watch her while she refilled the large coffee urn.

"I love this inn, Travis," Kristen said when she had finished her dry toast and the other guests were gone. "Did you see the roses?"

"Yeah." He sensed she was looking for more and smiled. "The roses are beautiful. But don't you want to go somewhere warm? I'd rather just hop on a plane to some tropical island and bask in the sun. That's what a honeymoon is supposed to be."

He saw Gena's shoulders tense, and he wondered whether it was the talk of his marriage or his trying to talk Kristen out of the Riverside Inn that bothered her.

It was a ridiculous question and he knew it. There was no reason for Gena to care if he got married. They were virtually strangers. But she knew that he was going to convince Kristen to choose a new location, so that didn't make sense either.

"I don't want to go that far from the studio," Kristen insisted. "This place is perfect. We're having an autumn wedding, and the leaves are so beautiful in the fall here. As a matter of fact, I've decided to hold the ceremony here as well, not just the reception and our honeymoon. The wedding party can stay here, and the guests can stay at hotels in the area. It will be smaller—more intimate."

Gena held her breath, waiting for Travis's reply. He had to see it was time to nip Kristen's ideas in the bud. A party and honeymoon were one thing, but a man simply didn't get married in his ex-wife's house. That was a little *too* intimate.

Travis said nothing, so Kristen continued, her voice making it clear that Travis should just smile and nod. "We'll have a Justice of the Peace perform the ceremony outside under a canopy if the weather's good, and in the front parlor if it's not. Then we'll have the reception, the guests will leave, and we'll spend a few days in that beautiful suite—with that amazing bathtub."

The suggestion in her voice put Gena's teeth on edge. It was quite clear what Kristen meant by that, and she didn't want to hear about it—much less allow it.

There is no way I'm going to let this happen. She turned, ready to speak, but Travis's look stopped her. He shook his head slightly, and she got a perverse sense of pleasure out of knowing he was scared she would blurt out the truth.

Maybe it was because she was so tired. Half the night she spent tossing and turning, replaying again and again her conversation with Mia. There were so many things she should have said and done differently. Not just last night, but for the last fifteen years. And she didn't know how to fix it.

The other half of the night she'd spent thinking about the man sleeping under her roof. When she was younger she would lie awake at night, picturing Travis's face—imagining his voice. She had fantasized about doing things she knew so little about, always with him.

The reality had been very different from the fantasy, and that's what Gena kept telling herself. But it didn't stop his face from filling her mind at all hours since his arrival.

"We don't have to decide right now," Travis said, pushing his empty plate away.

Gena smiled at him. They both knew the wedding would take place anywhere but in New Hampshire, but there was no reason she couldn't make him sweat a little. "You should decide soon if you have your heart set on an autumn wedding. When all the leaf-peepers come up to see the foliage we fill up quickly. You've already left it pretty late as it is."

"I think I've made up my mind," Kristen said, and Travis glared at Gena. "I know I have, actually. I'll need to spend some time contacting local caterers and florists, of course, but I'll give you a deposit before we leave tomorrow."

"Doesn't my opinion count?" Travis asked in a voice that was probably meant to sound joking, but came out angry.

"Of course not," Kristen said firmly. "Everybody knows it's the bride's day. And since this is the first wedding for both of us, it should be really special."

Gena felt a sharp pang of guilt. Hastily she grabbed the tray she used to carry the dirty dishes and went into the kitchen. She already knew Kristen didn't know about their marriage, but somehow hearing her gush about first weddings made her feel dirty and deceitful.

Well, it's not my place to tell her. When Travis showed up at City Hall with a divorce decree with her name on it they could fight it out between themselves.

The phone rang and Gena dropped the tray on the table with a clatter and grabbed the receiver. *Please be Mia...please...* "Hello?"

"Good morning, my name is Tim, and I'd like to save you money on your next long-distance calling bill."

Gena hung up the phone without saying a word, her eyes filling up with tears. She just wanted to know how she was doing. Mia said she would call, and she was trying so hard to respect that, but if her daughter didn't talk to her soon she was going to have a nervous breakdown.

She knew their relationship would survive this. Mia was just hurt and angry and she had every right to be. But they would get through it together, just as they always had.

Right now she was anxious to know what Mia had decided to do about Travis. Did she want to meet her father? Would she wait until he went back to Boston and call him when Kristen wasn't likely to be around? What would they do if Mia just came home and introduced herself to them?

Pain throbbed in Gena's temples and she wished she could just hide in the kitchen until Travis Ryan and his fiancée went away. Then she and her daughter could go back to their regularly scheduled lives.

"Why don't you go for a walk or something?" Kristen said when Travis pushed back from the table. "I want to make some calls—try to get recommendations for the local services we'll need."

"You can do that from Boston," Travis said, hooking his arms around her waist and pulling her close. "This weekend is supposed to be about relaxing and spending time with each other."

She flinched her shoulder in a very subtle, too familiar brush-off. "No, this weekend is about not leaving wedding details until the last minute. You heard Gena—I've already waited too long as it is."

He looked down at her face, each feature perfect in its own right, and stunning when taken all together. But he didn't like this look. He hated the cold and demanding green gaze, the perfectly arched brow. When her lips tightened, no amount of makeup could hide the lines that formed around her mouth.

It was a look that said *I'm somebody and you will do what I want.* And it was a look he saw often. If she wanted Thai and he wanted pizza. If he wanted to stay in when she had opera tickets. Pouting was not for Kristen Sinclair.

Imperious, he thought. That's the word that best described her. And he wasn't in the mood for it.

"Fine. You do whatever you want. Spend the whole damn weekend on the phone if you want to. But don't think I'm going to be right here watching TV, waiting for your summons."

"Where are you going?"

Travis paused at the door. "You told me to go for a walk."

"Don't be gone long." She had realized her mistake too late.

He didn't answer, but the stained glass shook in the door when he closed it behind him.

The hot sun and fragrant summer breeze washed over him, soothing his raw nerves and he immediately regretted losing his temper. He thought about going back to soothe her ruffled feathers, but she no doubt already had her cell phone pressed to her ear.

A walk would do him good right now anyway. He had plenty to think about, and he wasn't really in the mood to deal with either of the women in the house.

It was a short walk to downtown along the river. Flowers lined the sidewalk, no doubt planted and tended by a committee made up of the town's older ladies. The houses and lawns along the way were all well kept.

Main Street was lined on both sides by blocks of old, intricately detailed brick buildings, each of which housed several businesses. He wasted some time in the gift shops, then the gallery showcasing local artisans.

It was hard for Travis to believe fifteen years had passed since he'd seen the town. Very little had changed. There was a new gas station at the end of the block, and a video rental store that he wished had been there when he was a kid. But Frank Castille was still cutting hair and Smitty's no doubt still served up the best breakfasts for a hundred miles.

Travis bought an ice cream cone at the corner store, something he hadn't done in a very long time. If he was going to be forced to walk down memory lane, at least he could enjoy himself a little. A new park had been built to house the town's old statues, and he sat on a granite bench to watch the people go by.

It was a charming little town, full of people who knew almost everything about each other. A place where the people who lived on either side of you were truly neighbors.

But not a good town to get married in. He refused to let that thought darken his renewed good spirits. He'd find a way to convince Kristen that the Riverside Inn was not a good choice for their wedding and reception, and certainly not for their honeymoon. Maybe he'd just put his foot down and say no.

He didn't need an excuse. Regardless of what Kristen thought, it was his wedding, too. He just wished she hadn't pointed out that it was the *first* wedding for each of them. Not correcting her might only be a lie of omission, but it was still a lie. He didn't like being dishonest with her.

And thoughts of dishonesty brought him back to Gena. He had noticed that mischievous sparkle in her eyes when she disputed his claim that they didn't need to decide right away. She knew they wouldn't be getting married at the Riverside Inn. He'd made that very clear, and she had agreed. Still, she had him scared there for a second, and one look at her face told him she had done it purposely just to make him suffer.

Where was that fire fifteen years ago? Maybe it had always been there, and he had just been too young and too stupid to see it. It was hard for him to believe that such a captivating woman had been concealed under the baggy clothes and bad haircuts.

That thought shook him so badly he almost dropped his ice cream. Did he really think she was captivating?

Yes, he acknowledged grudgingly. Gena Taylor was captivating. She was beautiful and intelligent, and she didn't feel the need to make herself look artificial. He only wished he'd seen it sooner. About fifteen years sooner, because now it was too late. Tomorrow night he would get in the car and exit her life again.

I wish I had seen it sooner? That had to be exhaustion speaking. He refused to believe he was feeling…was it regret? It couldn't be, because walking out on that farce of a marriage was one of the smartest things he'd ever done.

Two teenaged girls walking toward the park caught his eye. One of them was upset, frowning and making choppy gestures with her hands as she spoke. Something tugged at his subconscious, and he thought there was something very familiar about the girl. He just couldn't place it.

Maybe she was the daughter of one of his old school friends. She'd be about the right age. Fifteen, he guessed.

Suddenly his mind produced the memory of a picture. It took another second to place the image. The photograph was of a young blonde woman cradling a baby on her lap. He was the baby and the woman was his mother.

The girl and her friend drew closer and he matched her features with those in the picture. The thick blonde curls...heart-shaped face...the eyes. He saw that distinct shade of blue when he looked at his mother...or in a mirror.

The girl's resemblance to that picture—to himself—was too uncanny to ignore, and he stood, black raspberry ice cream dripping unnoticed onto his hand.

Fifteen... She looked straight at him before her friend pulled her into the store, piercing him with her blue gaze. *Fifteen...my mother...oh my God.*

He dropped the ice cream in the grass and started running up the hill toward the Inn.

Gena could hear Travis shouting her name before he even entered the house. *He knows—somehow—he knows.* She was upstairs, but she heard the loud echo of his footsteps and the slamming of doors as he looked for her.

She was down the stairs and in her private living room when the door flew open and Travis was there. His chest heaved from anger and exertion, and Gena trembled in anticipation of his rage.

She watched him look around, saw his gaze fall on the school portrait of Mia that hung over the sofa.

"Who is that?" he demanded in a hoarse voice, pointing at the picture.

Gena swallowed and lifted her chin. "That's Mia—my daughter."

She saw Kristen appear behind Travis, her forehead wrinkled in confusion. "Travis? What's wrong? Why are you shouting?"

"She's my daughter, isn't she?"

"What? What is going on here?" Kristen demanded, but they both ignored her.

Gena's hands fisted at her sides. "She's *my* daughter. You left, remember?"

"Why didn't you tell me you were pregnant?" he shouted.

"Having a baby was the reason we got married, or did you forget that part?" Gena yelled back in a volume that matched his.

He was advancing slowly toward her, his face white with anger, and she backed up until she felt the seat of the rocker hit behind her knees. "You were lying. I saw the proof."

"No," Gena said in a more reasonable, but no less shaky voice. "What you saw was proof that I had some spotting."

Shannon Stacey

"Spotting?" Travis repeated, throwing his hands up. "What the hell is that supposed to mean?"

"Travis," Kristen snapped in a voice that demanded his attention. "I want to know what you're talking about, right now."

"Gena is my ex-wife."

"Oh, I got that part. And the child part. What I want to know is why I'm just hearing about this now."

"We didn't want to ruin your weekend," Gena explained quietly. "We thought it would be best just to go our separate ways on Sunday with nobody the wiser."

"*We* thought?" Kristen repeated. "Just what—"

"Kristen," Travis interrupted. "You and I can talk about this later. Right now I need to hear about my daughter."

My daughter. The words hit Gena like a fist in the gut, and she almost doubled over from the pain.

Those were the words she had feared hearing those first couple of years after the divorce. The way he said it—fierce and possessive—when he had yet to even meet Mia shook her to the core.

Her daughter would never belong solely to her again. And now that it was too late, she wasn't sure she wanted to share.

She watched the battle of emotions playing out across Kristen's face. No doubt she wanted to rant and rave—demanding answers—but Travis's expression clearly said that wouldn't be a good idea. He was focused on one thing—his daughter.

"Fine," Kristen snapped. "I'm going to pack and then I'm going back to Boston. You can go to hell."

She spun and walked away. Travis watched her go, then ran his hands over his face and through his hair. "Spotting...what is that?"

Gena took a deep breath, hoping some of the flame would leave her cheeks. "Just a little bleeding. Sometimes it happens in a pregnancy, especially if the woman is stressed or sick. I was both actually, but the doctor told me everything would be okay as long as I took it easy. You didn't know I saw the doctor because I had my mother drive me."

Travis sat on the edge of the sofa, his head in his hands. His face was pale and she watched the muscles in his jaw work as he clenched and unclenched his teeth. "Why didn't you tell me?"

She knew he was talking about more than the doctor visit. "Tell you what, Travis? That—yes, I was pregnant and we were going to spend the rest of our lives the way we spent those thirteen days? With me crying and you swearing and slamming doors?"

"Maybe it would have gotten better," he said, but he didn't sound as if he believed it any more than she did.

"No. You hated me so much, Travis. And I...well, I had always wanted to be your wife, just not like that. I wasn't any happier than you were."

"But after...dammit, Gena." He looked like a man whose entire world had just blown up in his face.

Her knees were trembling so much she was afraid she would collapse, so Gena sank into the rocking chair. "I should have told you, but I was scared."

"Scared of what?" Travis shouted, making an angry, sweeping gesture with his hand. "You'd already done the hard part. You confessed that you were pregnant, and our parents pushed us to get married. What could be scarier than that?"

"I was afraid that if we got divorced after the baby came your parents would take her away. You guys had everything—more money, a better house…"

They were silent for a few minutes, both of them trembling, and Gena close to tears. This wasn't the way she wanted to tell him. And how would she explain this to Mia? She would think she had driven him away purposely if he left before she got to meet him.

"Does she know about me?" he asked, and she felt a shiver of unease at the way his words mirrored her thoughts.

"I told her last night."

"That's why you were crying. She didn't take it well?"

Gena stared at him, confused. "You knew I was crying?"

"I was on the porch when you got home. You didn't see me. And the fact that I thought about comforting you at the time makes me sick right now." He paused, shaking his head as if he was having an inner dialogue with himself. "What did she say?"

"She thought we got divorced before I found out I was pregnant, and then I couldn't find you."

"You told her that? And she believed you? But then, you always were a good liar."

"I didn't lie!" she shouted. "I told you I was pregnant and I was. I didn't ask you to walk out."

"You didn't go out of your way to make me stay either, did you?" One of his hands clenched and unclenched over and over. "Back to my daughter. She believed you?"

"She was young," Gena explained. "But she found you somehow—on the internet, I guess—and she called your office."

The blood seemed to drain from Travis's face. His blue gaze bored into her own. "She tried to call me?"

"Your secretary wanted her name, so she panicked and hung up."

"She was looking for me and you *still* didn't say anything? What kind of mother are you?"

She didn't answer right away. *Be calm*, she was telling herself. She had to remember Mia. "I didn't know she was looking. It was her secret until last night."

He stood and started pacing the length of the room. An image of Mia doing the same superimposed itself in her mind and her throat swelled. How could her daughter be so much like this man she didn't even know?

"Her name is Mia? She's fifteen?"

"Mia Dawn Taylor," Gena said softly. "Yes, she's fifteen, and yes—she's yours. Where did you see her?"

"Downtown. I was sitting on a park bench and she was walking toward me with a friend. It took me a second to realize she looks just like my mother, and then it all clicked."

"The reason I told her last night was because I'd already decided to tell you. I just had to tell her first, and she asked for a little time to take it all in before I did."

"You're fifteen years too late," he snapped.

Gena stood so she could face him eye to eye. "What difference would it have made if I *had* told you then? You made it perfectly clear you didn't want us."

"No...I didn't want *you*." He turned and left without seeing the hurt in Gena's eyes.

Chapter Four

Travis tossed his toothbrush and electric razor into the suitcase, then zipped it closed. Kristen's luggage was already lined up at the door. She stood in the window, staring at anything but him.

"Kristen, I didn't know that Gena owned the Riverside Inn, and I didn't know about Mia. If I had I would have told you. You have to believe I didn't do this on purpose."

"When were you going to tell me you were married once before?" she asked without turning around.

It was the question he had been dreading, and he didn't have a good answer. "When the time was right, I guess."

"You mean when we went to get the license, right? We've been together four years, Travis. The right time has come and gone."

Travis sighed and picked up her big suitcase. "Let's talk about this at home when we've both had a chance to calm down. I can't do this right now."

"I don't think we'll do this at all," she said quietly, grabbing the smaller suitcases. "You should have told me."

"It's not something I'm proud of."

She pierced him with her green gaze. "From what I heard you shouldn't be."

"What the hell is that supposed to mean?"

"You found evidence your pregnant wife was bleeding and you *left* her?" She ran a careless hand through her usually perfect hair. "That's not you, Travis."

"It wasn't like that."

"Then what was it like?"

Travis set down her suitcase and started to pace. "Yes, I was drunk and stupid and had sex with her. The next thing I know she's pregnant and our parents are dragging us into the courthouse. I didn't even *know* her, and everybody kept telling me she'd done it purposely.

"She'd had a crush on me for years. Everybody knew it, and it made sense. I was young and angry and when I saw that blood on her underwear... What the hell do I know about pregnancy? It was too easy to believe she'd not only trapped me, but lied, too. I ran like hell."

Kristen shook her head. "You didn't even confront her? And what kind of backward-thinking parents force their child to get married because of a pregnancy?"

"Ours. It's a small town, and it was important to them. It was like a nightmare I couldn't wake from. I've never been proud of it, Kristen, but this...I didn't know."

She took a deep breath, her shoulders shuddering, and Travis reached out to comfort her. After jerking away, she picked up the smaller of her bags and started for the door. "I can't believe you never told me about this."

When he opened his mouth to speak, she held up her hand. "We'll talk in the car, Travis. Right now we're leaving."

They went through the house, nodding a goodbye to the other guests, and out to the porch. He hauled the luggage down the steps and set it next to the car. Then he froze.

Mia stood in the driveway, her hands shoved deep in her pockets. She was just standing there—staring—and Travis knew he didn't have to tell her who he was.

"Hi," was all he could think of to say, and he was aware of Kristen stiffening beside him.

"Hi."

Gena stepped out onto the porch and was stopped dead in her tracks by the sight of Travis and Mia. They were so alike. In their coloring, their build—even parts of their personality, though they didn't know it yet.

She watched them watch each other, each searching for the right thing to say. She was tempted to step in. She should introduce them, help smooth their meeting, but she stayed on the porch. So far she'd only managed to make things worse.

"I...I'm going back to Boston," Travis said.

"I can see that."

He wracked his brain for something—anything—to say. He spoke to teenagers all the time, but this one was different. She was his.

"When I saw you downtown I came home and talked to Gena—to your mother, I mean. What a mess, huh?"

Mia smiled, but it didn't quite reach her eyes. "Yeah, you could say that."

Another awkward silence, broken only by the thump of the suitcases Kristen was tossing into the trunk.

"I'm going to take Kristen home and do some juggling in the office on Monday. I'll be back here Tuesday evening."

Everybody froze, and even Travis was surprised by his own words. But he meant them. "I'll get a room near here, and maybe we can get to know each other a little. We can get a pizza or something."

This time the smile reached her eyes. "I'd like that. If it's okay with Mom."

Gena started to speak, but Travis cut her off. "It's not up to her. I *will* spend time with you as long as it's what you want. And I won't hesitate to get a lawyer if I need one."

He said the last words to Gena, and she recognized the challenge.

Her blood ran cold as her gaze swept over the Mercedes, his designer shirt, his leather shoes. Travis Ryan appeared to have deep pockets, and Gena probably couldn't even scrape up his pocket change. There was no doubt about who had the better lawyer.

She could fight him and maybe win—but she would probably lose her daughter in the process. Or she could move over and let him in.

One look into Mia's pleading eyes made the decision for her. The girl was desperate for a father—she knew that now—and she couldn't stand in her way. Not and live with herself later.

"You don't need a lawyer, Travis," she said, trying to not let her anger show in her voice. "There's no reason to make this any more complicated than it already is."

They all flinched when Kristen slammed the trunk lid down. "I've got to go," Travis said to Mia.

"Okay. I'll see you Tuesday."

Mother and daughter watched the Mercedes pull out of the drive, then they moved toward each other. Without a word Gena pulled Mia into her arms and held her there, not sure if she was comforting her daughter or herself.

"It'll be okay, Mom," Mia whispered. "I promise. You guys royally screwed up, but I still love you."

Gena laughed into her daughter's hair. "Have I ever told you what a dream you are?"

The following few days passed in a blur for Gena. She had guests come and go. There were the usual business affairs to take care of, but a part of her mind was always on Travis Ryan.

She kept replaying their confrontation over and over again, rethinking everything she'd said and analyzing every word he'd said, until she thought she'd go insane.

Mia was quiet, keeping her thoughts to herself. Gena knew the worst thing she could do was smother her. They were both tense, both lost in thought, and Gena felt the weight of her guilt like a stone around her neck.

But until Mia was ready to talk, there was nothing she could do to make it better. She wasn't sure she could *ever* make it better.

So when Jill Delaney called her before noon on Monday and asked her out to lunch, she jumped at the chance. She only had two guests—both were out for the day—and there was nothing pressing to demand her attention.

She needed a distraction—something to take her mind off Travis Ryan. He seemed to have taken up permanent residence in her thoughts, and it was driving her crazy. A change of scenery would do her good.

They arrived at the restaurant at the same time and grabbed a table. They both ordered coffee and decided to share a grilled chicken sandwich, but got a double order of fries.

"So, what's going on?" Jill asked when the waitress had taken their order and left.

"What do you mean?"

"Don't play dumb. Travis Ryan was spotted eating ice cream in the park on Saturday, and you are super tense. Plus you're snapping your fingernails together like mad."

Gena laughed and shook her head. "You're pretty smart for a blonde librarian."

"Blonde *children's* librarian, thank you, and being smart has nothing to do with it. I'm observant, and I've been your best friend forever. Now spill—did he see Mia?"

Gena sighed. Jill knew everything—she always had—and she'd never told a soul. "Yeah, he did. It was bad."

"And Mia knows?"

Gena told her the entire story, pausing only when the waitress brought their food, which they covered in salt, with plenty of ketchup for the fries.

"So he's coming back tomorrow?"

Gena nodded and shrugged, trying to ignore the little tingle in her stomach she felt every time she thought about seeing him again.

What's wrong with me? The man had threatened to sic his lawyer on her, and all she could think about was how much she loved the deep timbre of his voice—how much she wanted to run her fingers through his hair to see if it still felt the same after all these years.

"So, what are you going to do?" Jill asked.

"There's nothing I can do. He made it pretty clear he'll get a lawyer and take me to court if I try to stop him from seeing her. There is no way I can afford the kind of lawyer he can get."

"I can't believe he threatened you."

"He was angry," Gena replied. The words had barely left her lips when she felt a rush of disbelief. Why was she defending him?

"What if he tries to get joint custody?" Jill asked while she drenched the fries in more ketchup.

"I don't know. She's fifteen, though. I think a judge would leave it up to her at this point. But I really don't think Travis will do it if I don't try to keep him away."

They pondered the problem while finishing their lunch and second, then third cups of coffee. Neither of them could see a solution other than hoping for the best.

"It'll be good for Mia to have her father in her life, and you guys will work it all out, I promise," Jill said earnestly. "Just remember not to put Mia in the middle."

"I'll do my best not to," Gena said, staring into the bottom of her empty coffee cup.

"So, is he still cute?"

Gena felt the heat creeping into her cheeks and she wanted to crawl under the table. Whether or not Travis Ryan was still cute was not something she wanted to talk about. Even with Jill.

"You're blushing," Jill accused, a little too loudly. Several people turned to look at Gena, who sank lower into her seat. "Tell me about it."

"Yes, he's still cute, and he was also here with his fiancée, remember? They were planning their wedding," she reminded her.

"It doesn't sound like they'll be engaged long."

"Jill!" Gena was surprised that her very sweet, if sometimes scatterbrained, friend could be so catty. "Kristen was very nice, at least before she found out who I was, and I think they'll work it out. It was just a shock—to everybody involved."

"Do you hope they won't work it out?" Jill pressed, looking for a confession that Gena wasn't ready to give.

"It doesn't matter to me if they do or not. The only person I care about is Mia."

On that definitive, if not completely honest, note, they paid their bill and walked out into the noon sunshine. Jill gave her a quick hug , then left to return to the library.

Gena started the minivan and drove slowly back to the Inn. Jill's question kept running through her mind, and she couldn't seem to stop it. *Do you hope they won't work it out?*

The idea of Travis being single and available had its appeal, but she was smart enough to know there could never really be anything between them. There was too much history—too much animosity. And that was a mind game none of them needed to be involved in, especially Mia.

As long as Travis was with Kristen she didn't even need to think about it. He was off-limits, and Gena was perfectly fine with that.

Still, the memory of that long-ago night in Travis's pickup was surfacing more and more often of late. And last night, when she was half-asleep and that image popped into her head, the hands that pulled so urgently at her clothes and the face that pressed against her breasts had definitely belonged to the older Travis.

I am not going to develop a crush on my ex-husband, she tried to tell herself firmly.

Mia's words echoed in her mind. *It's not a crush. It's unrequited love.*

"No way," she said out loud. The last thing she was going to feel for Travis Ryan was *any* kind of love.

Travis drove north on 193, his thoughts flying through his head as quickly as the trees passing by his side window.

It wasn't until he drove through Concord that his palms started to sweat. In about thirty minutes he would see his daughter again. A fifteen-year-old stranger who had his eyes, his hair—his blood.

Even after several days it was still hard to believe he had a child. He had thought about having children in the future, but Kristen told him right up front that it would be years before she considered it. For the time being her career came first.

Now he was a father. Not of a helpless infant who would allow him to grow into being the father he thought he could be—but of a nearly grown young woman who had never had one. And he had no idea what she expected from him.

He'd been trying for the last two days to think of something to say to her—something more sensible than the flurry of questions that had been filling his head.

What was her favorite color? When did she lose her first tooth? He wanted to know what kind of music she listened to, how many boyfriends she'd had, if she had ever broken a bone. Did she play sports? What kind of grades did she get? How old was she when she walked? Did she suck her thumb like he did when he was a baby? Had some punk ever broken her heart?

She was all he had been able to focus on since he had seen her walking toward him on Main Street. And yet it was still so hard for him to believe.

During the frenzy of visits and phone calls necessary to prepare his practice for a week-long absence, Mia had constantly been in his thoughts. He hadn't even been able to concentrate on the problem of saving his engagement.

Kristen had not said a single word to him for an hour after leaving the Riverside Inn. Then she had yelled at him for twenty miles. She only stopped when he finally told her he would leave her off at the next rest stop if she couldn't discuss the situation like a reasonable adult.

She had really fallen into a sulk when he told her he was rearranging his schedule. After this week off he would be spending four days each week in New Hampshire. It wasn't until she realized she had to accept it or lose him that she came around. They'd talked for hours, working through the anger of the initial shock and agreeing, once they both grew accustomed to Mia's presence in their lives, they would be fine. The wedding plans would proceed, although the reception would definitely be in Boston.

Travis spotted a blue sign marking a rest area and pulled off the highway. He needed some fresh air, maybe a soda from the vending machines. Anything to calm his nerves.

"Mia Dawn Taylor," he said aloud as he walked toward the small information center. Saying her name was something he had done a lot in the previous days.

How could I not know? There was a part of him out there— growing, laughing, crying. And he had missed it.

Because of Gena. He slammed his hand against the Coke button on the machine, earning startled glances from a businessman and a weary-looking family.

He took his drink and walked back to the parking lot to sit on the tailgate of his pickup. All the while he tried to force down the bitter anger that rose whenever he thought of his ex-wife.

He still had a hard time grasping the fact that Gena had hidden his daughter from him for fifteen years. What if he and Kristen had married in Boston and never stepped foot in New Hampshire—never visited the Riverside Inn? The thought that he could have gone to his grave without ever knowing Mia existed made him sick to his stomach.

He wasn't without blame. He was ashamed of the way he'd used her, even then. Not knowing what to do about it, he'd hidden from her, avoided talking to her at all. He thought he'd done them both a favor by running and never looking back. Yes, his sins were many. But she'd taken his *child*.

Who the hell was she to decide whether or not he could be a father? Mia was his as surely as she was Gena's, and yet he had never read her a bedtime story or kissed a scraped knee.

And now he never would. It was too late. Mia was almost a woman grown, her days of being danced on Daddy's knee long over. When he thought of all that he'd missed—all the moments and milestones—he felt a surge of blazing anger at Gena.

Trapping him into marriage was small potatoes compared to stealing his daughter.

The sound of crinkling aluminum broke him away from his thoughts, and he was surprised to find he was crushing the can in his hand.

He had to get his emotions under control before he saw them again. Mia would be loyal to her mother, and his anger at her could scare the girl to the point she didn't want to see him.

How can I see Mia without seeing Gena? It was a question he couldn't answer, so he closed the tailgate and got back into his truck. He would know how it was going to turn out soon enough.

If she looks at that clock one more time I'm going to scream.

Although her fingers managed to draw out a map for Mr. Beauchamp, Gena's attention was squarely on Mia. The girl's growing excitement about seeing her father again was driving her crazy.

She had already changed her clothes twice, then applied makeup only to scrub it off. When she actually started pacing on the porch, Gena had told her to get behind the desk and file receipts.

"Make sure you watch for the orchard, then take a left. You can't miss it." She waited until Mr. Beauchamp left, then went to her daughter.

"He'll be here," she said, squeezing Mia's shoulders. "He said he would, so he will."

"And you'll be nice to him?"

Gena breathed deeply. "Yes, I'll be nice to him—for your sake. What happened between us has nothing to do with you."

"Yeah, right. What happened between you screwed up my whole life, remember?"

The all-too-familiar tears stung Gena's eyes and she pulled away. "Has it been that bad?"

She was relieved when Mia stood and threw her arms around her. "Stop it, Mom—" she squeezed hard "—you know I love you, and I'm sorry. I've been very happy—you know that. I was just...missing a piece."

"Well, your missing piece has turned up," Gena whispered into her hair. "And I won't do anything to drive him away. I promise."

"Thanks, Mom."

The sound of a vehicle pulling into the driveway broke them apart. Gena cursed under her breath when Mia rushed to the mirror, then the front door.

Travis Ryan was back in her life. And he wasn't leaving this time. He wouldn't walk out on them again. *But only because of Mia.*

Not that she cared. She was not going to let him affect her. If he stayed—good. And if he did leave, that would be fine, too. She had lived her life just fine without him, and she didn't need him now.

Now if her body would only get that message, she'd be doing even better. *It's only physical*, she scolded herself. Those little twinges in her heart were just echoes of the past. He had been her first, after all, and a girl never forgot her first.

That's all it was. And as long as she kept telling herself that, everything would be all right.

Travis turned off the ignition and stepped out of the truck, feeling more nervous than he ever had before a big game—even the championship hadn't made the butterflies swarm in his stomach like they were right now.

Mia stood on the porch, and he saw his own uncertainty reflected on her face. The poor kid looked scared to death, but still happy to see him, and Travis smiled up at her.

"Hi, Mia."

"Hi."

So far, so good, he thought wryly. He dealt with teenaged athletes almost daily, so he had thought he would be better prepared for this. But it was different. This girl was his *daughter*—his own flesh and blood.

"So…you ready for that pizza?" he asked in a tremulous voice, wondering if any situation he'd ever been in had been as awkward as this.

"Sure," Mia replied, and her face lit up when she smiled, just like his mother's did.

Travis marveled anew at the resemblance. Kristen had pushed him to have a DNA test performed, but he didn't need a lab result to tell him he was Mia's father. It was so obvious to him that he was surprised she had even suggested it.

But there was more to it than her appearance. It just felt right to him. Despite Gena's history of lying, he knew in his heart this was true.

Gena's history, he thought. He reluctantly had to admit she hadn't lied and schemed her way into being Mrs. Travis Ryan after all. A small part of him could even sympathize with how scared and unhappy she must have been, but it was a *very* small part.

And this was the reason—he was standing in front of a girl for whom he should have been a knight in shining armor—a constant protector in the world. Instead she had grown up without him.

"Um...should I tell Mom we're leaving?" Mia asked, and he realized he'd just been standing there, staring at her.

"I'm going to speak to her for a minute, actually. If you're ready to go you can wait in the truck."

Gena heard him enter the house and she waited for him in the kitchen, her arms folded across her chest. This meeting would no doubt set the tone for their entire relationship, and though she knew she couldn't afford to put up a strong legal fight, she wasn't going to be a doormat, either.

The door swung open and she tried to stay calm, but she could feel the bright spots of color on her cheeks.

Travis spotted her, and her stomach clenched when she saw the way his jaw tightened. "Hello, Travis."

"Gena," he said tightly. "I'm taking Mia out for pizza, and I don't know how long we'll be."

"Take your time," she said. "I know you probably have a lot to talk about, and she's out of school for the summer, so she can stay out a little late."

He ran a hand through his hair, and Gena couldn't keep herself from watching his fingers slide through the thick blonde strands. "Look, about the other day—I shouldn't have threatened you with a lawyer. Not that I won't get one if you try to keep me from seeing her, but it was a little…premature."

"I won't keep you from seeing her. Not unless Mia asks me to, and I don't think she will. She's been watching the clock since you left on Saturday."

"So have I," he said, and she thought she saw the smallest glimmer of a smile.

"I'm sorry about all this, Travis. I—"

The trace of a smile disappeared. "There's nothing you can say to make this better, Gena. Nothing can fix what you did, and I'm never going to forgive you for it."

She felt each word like a well-deserved lash across her conscience. Tears stung her eyes and she looked down, unable to meet his gaze.

"But—" he paused, sighed "—I've thought about this on the drive up. I want us to have a good relationship…for Mia's sake."

She nodded, but didn't trust herself to speak for a moment. Then she cleared her throat and said, "That's what I want, too."

"Good. I'm staying at the hotel over by the highway, and I wrote down my room number and the telephone number." He handed her a business card which she dropped on the counter without reading. "Starting next week I'll be in Boston Mondays through Wednesdays, and I'll be here from Wednesday night to Sunday night."

"Kristen must not like that," Gena said, wishing immediately she could take the words back. She sounded like she was trying to find out if his relationship with his fiancée had survived the weekend, and she didn't want him to think she cared.

"She doesn't, but we'll work it out."

That answers that question. Not that she was asking. He'd already made it perfectly clear how he felt about her, and even if she wanted to, she probably couldn't change his mind.

He looked tired, and the pangs of guilt that had been her constant companions since Saturday returned with a vengeance. Fifteen years ago she had done what she thought was the right thing, but now, seeing what she had done to Travis made her wonder if they could have worked it out.

No, she thought. It had been the right thing to do. Maybe not for Mia, but definitely for herself. There was no doubt that if she had stopped him from leaving, they would all have needed more therapy than they could afford.

The kitchen door opened and Mia stuck her head in. "It's pretty hot in the truck. You almost done?"

Travis laughed nervously and nodded. "We're done. Sorry about that."

"Have a good time," Gena said and smiled at her daughter.

Suddenly Travis couldn't swallow and his breath caught in his chest. That was the smile—the smile he had remembered for years after that night in his truck.

He would never forget the sweet smile Gena had given him while he took her virginity. For years he had looked for it on the faces of other women, but he never found it. Not even Kristen smiled at him that way.

Gena had deserved so much better than the little of himself he had given her. He wished for a moment that he could go back to that night. He wanted to be worthy of that smile, to deserve her...love.

It *was* love that turned the corners of her lips up like that and softened her gaze. He wanted to bask in the warmth of that look again. There was no doubt she had loved him then, and he had thrown it away.

And she took my daughter from me. She got her revenge. The anger washed over him like an ice-cold shower, and he followed Mia to his truck without saying goodbye to her mother.

Chapter Five

After several weeks of standing at the window and watching Travis pick up and drop off Mia, Gena managed to convince herself that what she had felt for Travis Ryan was nothing more than an echo of a young girl's dreams.

So what if her heart started hammering in her chest the second she heard his truck pull in to the driveway? And those nights she spent tossing and turning, reliving the way he had looked at her in the kitchen just before the angry mask slipped back into place meant nothing.

I've just been lonely lately, she told herself while she stripped one of the guest beds. *None of it means anything.*

She heard Mia calling for her and stepped out into the hall. "I'm up here, honey."

Her daughter bounded up the steps, her face glowing with good news. "I just got off the phone with Dad."

Gena could almost hear that word without feeling a pinprick of guilt and jealousy. *Almost.*

"They want me in their wedding. I'm going to be a bridesmaid!"

The pinprick became a burning stab. "That's wonderful, sweetheart."

She hugged Mia, thankful for a reason to hide her face, even if only for a few seconds.

He's still getting married. Gena pressed her lips together and turned back into the guestroom when Mia let her go.

"Do you know what kind of dress you'll need?"

What did you think he was going to do—realize he had loved you all along and cancel his wedding? She wasn't good enough for him then and she wasn't good enough for him now.

She hated herself for even caring—even considering the possibility. Falling for Travis Ryan again would only land her in another big pile of heartbreak. It had taken long enough to dig herself out the last time.

Mia picked up the bundle of dirty sheets and shoved them into the basket. "Dad said that maybe next month I could spend a weekend with them in Boston. Then Kristen and I can go look at the dresses. She already has them picked out, but I'll need to be fitted.

"And they're going to get married in Boston, then go to the Virgin Islands for their honeymoon, which is what Dad wanted all along. And Kristen wants me to spend a week there before the wedding so that she can introduce me to her friends and family. That way there won't be any awkward questions during the wedding."

Gena listened to her daughter's breathless excitement and had to smile. Mia was happy—deliriously so—and that was what mattered. Anything else lived only in her imagination.

"And Dad said they would invite you to the wedding if I wanted them to."

That stopped Gena in her tracks. *Me—at Travis's wedding?* Watching Travis in his tuxedo pledging his undying love to a beautiful, wealthy woman wasn't high on her list of things to do. And no matter how logical she tried to be with herself, seeing him kiss the bride would rip her heart out. They had skipped that part at their wedding.

"Thank you, sweetie, but I'll pass."

Mia frowned and put her hand on her hip. "I knew you'd say that. I guess the wedding would be awkward, but you and Dad need to spend more time with each other. You're both my parents and there are going to be times you have to be together."

"And we'll do fine." She kissed her daughter's cheek and walked down the hall to the next room. "We won't have any trouble being polite to each other."

"I don't want you to just be polite. I want you to like him."

Gena bit down on a little burst of laughter. She wanted to say *I like him a little too much*, but she didn't. Her personal problems were just that—her own.

"I think he still likes you," Mia added, and there was no misreading her tone.

Gena tossed a dust rag at the girl. "Mia Dawn Taylor, don't you go getting any ideas in that head of yours. First of all, he can't *still* like me because he didn't like me then. And weren't you the one just talking about weddings and bridesmaid dresses?"

Mia sighed and made a half-hearted swipe over the dresser-top. "Yeah, but—"

"There is no *yeah, but*," Gena interrupted. "Look, your…dad and I might be able to manage a friendship, sweetie, but there will *never* be anything more.

"Travis is marrying Kristen in a few months, and it sounds like she's willing to accept—maybe even welcome—you as a part of their lives. You need to respect her and that includes not wishing her fiancé is attracted to his ex-wife."

She was surprised she could even get the words out, considering the thoughts she'd had over the past days. But what she told Mia was true, and she needed to start believing it herself.

A vehicle pulled in under the window and Gena frowned. She knew it was Travis's truck, and she hadn't known he was coming. Looking at Mia, she raised an eyebrow.

"That's Dad. When I was on the phone with him he asked if I wanted to go see a movie. Is that okay?"

"Considering the fact he's here now, it's a little late to ask," she replied with a wry smile. "But you need to finish dusting this room and carry the baskets down to the laundry room. I'll tell him you'll be right along."

Travis was halfway up the porch steps when the door opened. He smiled, expecting his daughter, then froze when he saw it was Gena standing in front of him.

God, she's beautiful, was his first thought, and he mentally kicked himself—again.

He had to stop thinking about her. The mixture of anger and lust he felt whenever he did was making him crazy. But she looked so good to him right now. She wore denim shorts and a T-shirt from the Speedway, and her ponytail was coming loose, letting wisps of auburn hair blow around her face.

Her legs were long and tanned, and he imagined her spending hours in the sun tending the garden. And he could hardly help the way the bold letters emblazoned across the front of her T-shirt drew his eye.

What he couldn't understand was how his body could betray him by responding to a woman that common sense told him he should despise.

"Hello, Gena," he said, careful to use a neutral tone. "I asked Mia to see a movie with me."

She nodded. "I wanted to talk to you about that."

He felt disappointment, followed quickly by anger. "You're not going to let her go?"

"I didn't say that," she said quickly. "I just think you should ask *me* first."

Travis walked slowly up the last steps and across the porch until he was looming over her. "You told me you wouldn't keep me from seeing her."

She put her hand on his chest and tried to shove him back, but he didn't move. "Don't try to intimidate me again, Travis Ryan. And don't put words in my mouth."

He grasped her hand, intending to push it away. But he held it, gripping it far tighter than he'd intended.

Her skin was hot, and as he watched a red flush creep up her neck, he wondered if she had a fever or if she was just that angry at him.

Travis moved his fingers, feeling the fine bones in her small hand. He watched in fascination as the flush in her face gathered into two bright spots of color high on her cheeks. His eyes slid down to her mouth, finding her lips parted slightly as her breaths became faster and more shallow.

Don't do it, he told himself, even as he wondered what she would do if he lowered his head just a little bit more, if he tasted her lips.

"Mia," Gena said quickly.

He didn't know if it was a warning that she was coming or a reminder of what they were talking about, but whatever it was—it worked. He dropped her hand and took a step back. He wasn't sure his voice would work right at the moment, so he just lifted an eyebrow, waiting for her to say something.

"I...um...I'm not saying you can't see her. I just would like for you to ask me first. Or have her ask me. She has responsibilities here, and I—I'm still her...custodial parent. Mia works here at the Inn, and she gets paid for it. I rely on her help and she can't just go running off whenever she feels like it. And we need to establish some boundaries—a routine—before school starts again."

He had to admit she was right. She had been Mia's sole parent for fifteen years. And even though being a single parent had been her own decision, it wouldn't be good for him to throw her rules and discipline out the window. He didn't want Mia to like him just because he was the *fun* parent.

"Okay," he said simply, and he smiled at the surprise on her face. "I understand what you're saying, and I agree with it."

"Thank you. And stop thinking I'm going to try to keep you away from her. That's not going to happen."

"I think it's a pretty reasonable fear. After all, you've done it once, haven't you?" He regretted the words almost as soon as he said them, but he wouldn't take them back. If nothing else it served to remind his heart of what his mind never forgot. This woman was off-limits.

She stared at him for a long moment, and he saw the hurt and guilt in her eyes. "Mia will be right out."

She turned and walked back into the house. He almost stopped her, but it wouldn't do any good. There was nothing either of them could say to change the past.

"I can't believe I let you talk me into this," Gena said the following night.

"Mom, it's just one night," Mia said, dropping two rented movies on the coffee table. "It'll be fun."

"Fun? Eating pizza and watching movies with my ex-husband?" Gena shook her head and set the napkins and paper plates next to the movies.

"Why don't you think of him more as my dad and less as your ex-husband?" She smiled when Gena rolled her eyes. "Come on—it's a family night."

But we're not a family. It was becoming more and more clear to Gena that's exactly what Mia was after. Somehow she had gotten the idea that her parents would make a great couple.

"Can't we do it another night?" Maybe when what happened on the porch made a little more sense.

"It has to be tonight. Dad's only in town from Wednesday nights to Sunday nights, and we have guests this weekend. It's the only night we haven't been booked in a long time."

"It will be great," Mia continued when Gena remained silent. "It'll give you guys a chance to get to know each other better."

Gena turned and gave her daughter a stern look. "You're not a little girl anymore, so I'm going to make this plain. Your father and I will never be more than civil to each other. There's too much pain and too much blame for the past, and we will *not* be romantically involved.

Travis is getting married to Kristen, and I'm very happy with my life, and that's the end of it."

Mia just shrugged and went to the kitchen for plates, leaving Gena to stare after her. She had seen that shrug many times before and she knew what it meant. It was Mia's way of saying *we'll see.*

The doorbell rang and Gena took a deep breath. She could make it through one evening. They would be watching movies, eating, and talking to Mia. They wouldn't be alone, like they had been on the porch.

Where he almost kissed me yesterday. She had seen the look in his eyes, and he looked like a man who was about to do something he knew he shouldn't. And she had wanted that kiss—yearned for it. But it would only lead to more heartbreak and she knew it. So she had thrown Mia's name out there, hoping it would remind him of how much he didn't like her. It had worked—maybe a little too well.

She heard Mia and Travis in the kitchen, so she pasted on a smile and went out to say hello.

The words almost got caught up in her throat, but she swallowed hard and squeezed them out. "Hello, Travis."

He was fresh from the shower. His blonde hair was still darkened from being slightly damp, and it curled a little over his ears. His skin glowed from a scrubbing, and his freshly-shaved jaw looked as smooth as silk despite its strong edge.

"I got pepperoni and bacon," he said, giving her what looked to be a genuine smile. "I've never had it, but Mia says I'm missing out."

They followed her into their private living room and Travis set the pizza box on the table where the plates and several cans of soda already sat. Mia popped the first movie into the VCR, then sat in the rocking chair, a tiny smile playing along the corners of her mouth.

Gena glared at her daughter, but she was being deliberately ignored. With the rocking chair occupied, that left only the small sofa for Travis and Gena. The *very* small sofa—more of a loveseat, really.

She sat and Travis did the same, seemingly as reluctant as she was. She was aware of how close his thigh was to her own, how easy it would be for her arm to brush against his. It was going to be a long few hours.

Gena stared at the television screen, but she didn't see the opening credits or the car chase that followed them. The only thing her mind could register was the heat of Travis's body next to her, so close she could smell his soap—the warm, spicy scent of his skin.

She could hear each breath he took, and judging by how rigid he looked from the corner of her eyes, he wasn't totally engrossed in the movie either. She would gladly have given more than a penny for his thoughts at that moment.

There was no way she could ask him. Even if she could gather the courage to ask him what he was thinking about right then, she couldn't very well do it with Mia sitting right there. And she wasn't sure she wanted to know the answer.

"Aren't you guys going to have some pizza?" Mia asked, reaching for her second slice.

Gena's appetite was gone. She was sure the food would taste like sawdust in her mouth, but she took a slice anyway. Woodenly, she took bite after bite, not even trying to follow the complicated plot of the movie.

We're never doing this again, she fumed silently. She would just have to explain to Mia that she and Travis both wanted to be with her, just not at the same time. No more family nights, because there was no family. There was a mom and there was a dad and a daughter who belonged to each of them, but not together. And the sooner Mia realized that, the easier Gena's life would be.

Travis tried to concentrate on the movie, but it was too damn hard with Gena sitting so close to him that he could hear her breathing.

Sometime during the night, while he was lying awake staring at the ceiling, he had finally stopped trying to kid himself. He wanted Gena. Wanted her like he hadn't wanted a woman in a very long time—if ever.

Despite the past, despite the lies—even despite the fact he had come so close to never knowing Mia—he felt an urge to take her in his arms and kiss her senseless.

But then he remembered the tone of Kristen's voice when he talked to her, *after* he had almost kissed his ex-wife on the front porch. His fiancée was an intuitive person and somehow she knew she was losing him. Hurting her was the last thing he wanted to do, but he couldn't let her go. Not when he wasn't even sure his reaction to Gena wasn't caused by his own needs. Kristen worked a hectic schedule, and there wasn't a lot of time for him. And for all he knew it could be some psychological need to return to his teenage years.

Gena shifted next to him, and he caught a scent of her—Ivory soap, fruit-scented shampoo, a hint of perfume. She put her feet up on the coffee table, her arm resting at her side. Without thinking about the consequences, Travis slid his arm over just a bit and took her hand in his.

He heard her quick intake of breath, but she didn't pull away. He waited, keeping his eyes on the TV screen, until she relaxed, then he moved his thumb lightly across her palm.

Hidden from Mia's view by the tent of Gena's knees, he drew tiny circles on her palm, holding back his smile when she shivered almost imperceptibly. With his thumb and forefinger he slid up the length of each of her fingers, then returned to tickling the sensitive flesh in the center of her hand.

Gena stared straight ahead, willing herself to pull her hand away, but she couldn't do it.

Each stroke of his thumb across her palm stoked the fire burning deep in the pit of her stomach. It was a flame that had been neglected for far too long, and she couldn't bring herself to douse it yet.

He played idly with her fingers, caressing each one in turn. She closed her eyes for just a second, imagining him lifting her hand to his mouth, flicking his tongue over each fingernail, drawing each finger into the moist warmth of his mouth in turn.

Desire welled up deep within her, and she knew once she went down this path she couldn't turn around again. She didn't care. She wanted him.

There was no question now that her heart was going to be broken. More than broken—it would be shattered.

Still she couldn't pull away, until Mia stood suddenly. "I'm going to microwave some popcorn. Be right back."

Gena jerked her hand out of Travis's as if she'd been burned. He lifted his hand to push back his hair while she dropped hers in her lap.

With her heart in her throat, she watched her daughter walk out of the room and close the door behind her. She was trembling so hard the strands of hair around her face shook.

Travis cleared his throat and she turned to face him, her cheeks burning from embarrassment and the remnants of desire. "What do you think you're doing?"

"I don't know—" he hooked his hand behind her head and pulled her close "—but it's not good."

Gena told herself to push him away, to tell him that she wasn't interested in whatever his intentions were. But his objective was made perfectly clear as he lowered his face to hers. Then she didn't want to stop him anymore.

Her eyelids slid closed as his lips brushed hers, and she felt the first sharp pain of heartbreak. His fingers tightened in her hair and his mouth pressed harder against hers, demanding she respond.

With a sigh she gave in. Pushing away all thoughts of reason and consequences, Gena opened her mouth to him, tasting the soda's sweetness on his lips.

His tongue brushed across hers and she shuddered, turning her body toward him. Gena ran her hand up Travis's arm, reveling in the feel of the taut muscles under her fingertips. The clean, spicy scent of him filled her senses and she clutched his shoulder, her fingernails biting into his cotton T-shirt.

Travis nipped at her bottom lip and she moaned softly. He deepened the kiss, devouring her, and she responded in kind. She plunged her hand into his hair, letting the dense strands slide through her fingers. Her body strained against him, hungry for his touch.

His hand left her hair, sliding down to caress her neck, and each stroke of his fingers pulled at her core, drawing her deeper into the kiss.

The microwave door slamming closed jerked Gena back to reality. She pulled away from Travis, her breath coming in short, shallow pants.

His eyes seemed to reflect the turmoil she was feeling and she turned her face toward the television. She willed him not to say anything—not to pile any more humiliation on top of what she already felt.

"Gena, I…I'm sorry." From the corner of her eye she watched him run a hand over his face. "I shouldn't have done that."

"I shouldn't have let you."

What if Mia had stuck her head through the door to watch the movie while she waited for the popcorn to pop? The girl had enough fantasies about her parents being a couple without catching them making out on the couch like randy teenagers.

Travis cursed and shook his head. "I can't do this. I can't do this to Kristen—to you—to…myself."

Gena pinch her lips together, then said in a steady voice that surprised her. "I'm not going to play the role of the *other woman*, so it's not a problem."

"Did I ask you to?" he demanded, raising his voice enough that she shushed him.

"What do you call that…kiss?"

"A mistake," he said firmly. "A mistake I won't make again."

The conviction in his voice rocked her, turning some of her hurt to defensive anger. "You won't have the chance again."

They sat in tense silence while Mia came back and settled herself back in the rocker. She offered around the popcorn and Gena took a handful just to give herself something to do. The movie was almost over, and she hoped Travis would think of a good reason not to stay for the second one.

She wanted him gone, if only to make it easier for her to lie to herself. No matter what she had said to him, she wasn't sure she had the strength to tell Travis no if he tried to make the same *mistake* again. She could only pray he wouldn't.

⚜️

Travis watched the closing credits scroll by with a mixed feeling of relief and dread.

Somehow he had thought after meeting Mia that his life couldn't get any more complicated. He had been wrong. Kissing Gena had to be one of the dumbest things he had done since making love to her in his pickup back in high school.

Since having sex with her, he corrected himself. It had never been about love, and it wasn't now. It was attraction, plain and simple. He was a pretty good-looking guy and she was a beautiful woman. And it certainly didn't help that Kristen hadn't been feeling very affectionate lately.

Thinking about Kristen made him feel like a first-class heel. How was he going to explain this to her? He had promised to spend extra time with her this weekend. The original plan was for him to head out after the movies. He'd get back to Boston late, but he could get some sleep and have breakfast with her in the morning, then be ready for whatever her plans were when she got out of work in the evening.

But there was no way he could sit next to Gena for another two hours. Not with the taste of her still on his lips and the sweet scent of her filling his lungs.

He had to leave, and he would get in his truck and drive straight to Boston. He looked at his watch and calculated the time. He would find Kristen in her plush white robe, going over her notes for tomorrow's broadcast. She would be happy to see him, but slightly annoyed at the interruption. And a lot more annoyed when she heard what he had to tell her.

He stood and looked over at Mia. "Sorry, kiddo, but I've got to run a little early."

Her crestfallen look tugged at his heart, but he stood firm. "I promised Kristen I would spend some extra time with her and I've got to get back."

Mia smiled and shrugged. "Okay. You'll tell her I said hi, right?"

"Sure." He risked a glance down at Gena, but she was staring resolutely at the TV screen, her lips pinched tightly together. "And I have a late meeting on Wednesday, so I'll see you Thursday night, okay?"

He felt a little better when Mia walked over to give him a hug and a kiss on the cheek, but he was already dreading the night ahead.

Chapter Six

Later that night, Travis sat stiffly on Kristen's white leather couch, staring down at the empty whiskey tumbler in his hand.

She stood in front of the massive window, looking out at the lights of the city. "I'm going to cancel our reservations, and get back my deposit on the dress."

"Kristen, I..." He let the words trail off, then cursed. "You're going to throw away our future because of a kiss?"

She whirled to face him, her face white with anger. "This wasn't some floozy you picked up in a bar, Travis. You have a history with this woman, and it's not a pleasant one. And you still kissed her, so there has to be something there."

He opened his mouth, then closed it again and shook his head. He couldn't lie to her. He wasn't sure what was between him and Gena, but there definitely was something. But he couldn't explain it to Kristen when he didn't understand it himself.

He had only told her because he knew it was something he wouldn't be able to hide. Dishonestly was something he abhorred in others, and especially in himself. She would have known something was eating at him eventually, so it was best to be upfront about it.

She took a deep breath. "This has been a shock for everybody and I know your emotions are really out of whack right now, but I can only take so much.

"First the ex-wife and the daughter, then you're going to live up there four days of every week. Now you're kissing the woman who kept you from your child for fifteen years. I just don't understand this."

"I don't either," he said quietly, guilt burning his gut in a way the expensive whiskey couldn't touch. "I don't want to hurt you."

"Too late," she whispered, almost to herself.

Travis set the glass on the side table and stood, intending to hold her, convince her—and himself—this was where he truly belonged.

She held up her hand to stop him. "Don't even think about touching me, Travis."

"Kristen, I…I don't know what to say."

"Do you love me?"

"Yes." He did love her, and it was killing him to see the pain in her eyes—to know he had caused it.

"Do you love *her*?"

"N-no." *Love*? He didn't think love was what he felt for Gena. Desire, yes—but not love.

Kristen didn't miss the hesitation and she looked up at the ceiling, trying to hold back the tears. "I'm not marrying you."

"I—"

"But I'm not giving you up without a fight either," she interrupted. "You need to get your head back on straight and when you do, then we'll see if there's anything left of us."

"There will be," Travis said, and he meant it. What he felt for Gena wasn't real, and he wasn't going to throw away this woman's heart because of it.

"And you can sleep at your own place tonight."

࿓࿇ᯤᯤ

Gena was clearing the table of dirty dishes from a houseful of guests when the doorbell sounded.

She sighed and set down the tray, hoping it wasn't yet another spur of the moment traveler looking for a vacancy. Usually weekdays were slower, but people took longer weekends in the summer and Thursdays were being included in the bookings. She opened the door and was taken aback to find Travis there. She hadn't been expecting him.

She pasted on a smile. "Mia's not home. She has cheerleading camp this week. It's only days, so she'll be home by five."

"I know she's not here. She told me about the camp."

He was there to see her? Dread mingled with anticipation in the pit of her stomach, and her hands started to tremble. She remembered her resolve not to let him affect her and cursed herself for a fool.

"What do you want?" That sounded uninviting enough.

"We need to talk, Gena. There are some things we need to set straight."

"I'm pretty busy." She knew her smile was slipping, and she didn't want him to see her anxiety. "And I think things are straight enough."

Travis apparently disagreed because he stepped close to her, and when she backed away he walked by her into the house. "I have some things to say, and I don't want Mia around when I do."

"Fine," Gena snapped, knowing she couldn't win this battle. "We can talk in the kitchen."

She pulled out a chair for him, then went to lean on the counter at the far side of the room. She crossed her arms and waited to hear what he had to say, even though she really wasn't sure she wanted to.

"We need to talk about what happened the other night," he said, staring down at the table.

"Maybe you need to talk about it, but I don't." The last thing she wanted to do was rehash that kiss. She'd been doing enough of it on her own.

"Kristen and I aren't getting married in the fall."

Gena felt as if every nerve ending in her body had suddenly gone on high alert. *He's not going to marry her?* Her pulse quickened and she tried to think of something to say, but she failed and could only wait for him to continue.

"We're going to put it off for a while so I can sort some things out."

Gena let the air out of her lungs, disappointment making her teeth clench. *For a while? Sort some things out?*

Was she one of those things? She found it hard to believe Travis had run right home and told Kristen he had kissed her.

"Oh," was all she said.

"Maybe next year."

They were still together. She tried not to feel the hurt, but it came anyway. And it was especially painful after that brief moment of hope.

"Well," she said briskly, "I hope it all works out for you. But I have rooms to clean and baking to do, so if that's all…"

He looked up at her then, and some of her anger drained away. Having his life turned upside down was taking a toll on him, and he looked exhausted. She was nearly overwhelmed by an urge to walk over, wrap her arms around him, and soothe away the tension in his face. Only the danger of having him push her away kept her where she was.

"That's not all," he said, then ran his hand across his face. "My parents are coming up this weekend. They want to meet Mia, and they want to do it here. A show of family if you will."

"I've pretty much had it with the whole *family* thing," she told him.

"So have I, but it's one time. It'll be a couple of hours at the most."

He wasn't quite pleading, but she could hear in his voice that he didn't want it any more than she did. It would make his life easier if she just went along.

Not that she cared how easy his life was, but it would be good for Mia. And she could certainly stand two hours with her daughter, an ex-husband she was still in love with, and the former in-laws she had never liked in the first place.

Still in love with... The thought seemed to stick in her mind, playing over and over like a track from a scratched CD. It wasn't true, because she hadn't loved him before. She thought she did, but it hadn't grabbed hold of her heart the way it did now. She had been a girl then, with no idea of how it truly felt to love another.

No, I didn't love him then and I don't love him now, she reminded herself a little desperately. It was infatuation. That's all it had ever been. She had to believe that.

"Well?" he prompted impatiently.

"Saturday," she agreed quickly, before she had a chance to talk herself out of it. "Sundays can be busy sometimes with people checking out."

"Thanks, Gena. I'll call them tonight." Travis stood and started pacing, and her mind shied away from the subject he was working his way back around to.

He sighed and shoved his hands deep into his pockets. "Which brings us back to the...other night."

Unable to just stand and watch him pace, she picked up a sponge and started wiping down the spotless counter. "I'm not listening."

"About the kiss—"

"I told you I don't want to talk about that."

"Well, you don't have any choice," he yelled. "I'm not leaving here until you do."

She whirled and threw the sponge at him, feeling a quick rush of satisfaction when it left a wet rectangle on the front of his shirt.

"I do have a choice," she shouted. "I can throw you out of here and you can call your lawyer or your parents or the damn President for all I care. This is my home and you will respect me in it."

"I—"

"And furthermore—" she advanced slowly on him "—I am tired of you telling me what I'm going to do and what my daughter is going to do."

"We talked about that and you told me you wouldn't stop me from seeing her."

"I'm not talking about you seeing her. I'm talking about you coming in here like you're the head of this household. *I* am the head of this household and I have been since you walked out on us fifteen years ago."

His face flushed to a bright red and he pointed an accusatory finger at her. "That was your choice. All you had to do was open your mouth and say 'Hey, I *am* pregnant, stupid' and I would have stayed."

"And done what? Hated me forever? Drank yourself into oblivion watching college football on TV because it could have been you? Pardon me if that's not the life I wanted for me or my child."

Her words made him pause, the anger rushing out of him. He stared down at her, their chests rising and falling in almost perfect unison. *Is that what I would have done?*

It was, and he knew it. And he knew she must have been scared, but so very relieved when he did toss his ring on the table and leave. He remembered those thirteen days and how he had treated her, and even now, as angry as he was, he regretted it.

"I'm sorry," he said softly, and judging by the sudden wary look in her eyes, the words surprised her as much as they had surprised him.

"I am sorry," he said again. "I treated you so badly, and all I can say is that I was young and I was a jerk."

He watched her bottom lip start to tremble, and tears swell in her eyes before spilling over onto her cheeks. He tried to take her arm when she turned away, but she jerked free and sat down at the far side of the table.

"I had wanted to marry you since I was five years old," she said, swiping her hand across her eyes. "I thought you were my Prince Charming."

"Instead I turned out to be a frog." He sat back in his own chair and reached across the table to take her hand.

She didn't snatch it back as he thought she would. She just stared down at his fingers curled around hers, then smiled. "I called you much worse than a frog at the time. And you wouldn't even believe what my father called you."

He laughed. "I can imagine."

They were quiet for a minute, and Travis decided it would be dangerous to stay here in the kitchen with her for much longer. He was too comfortable and he could imagine all too clearly being curled up with her on the sofa in front of the fireplace, talking and laughing together while Mia did her homework.

But it's never going to happen, he reminded himself. His purpose in coming was to restore a friendly, platonic relationship with his child's mother—nothing more. Then he would marry Kristen and they would all live happily ever after. He was sure that's what he wanted.

Gena stared down at their hands, and she knew the smartest thing she could do was pull away, throw him out of the house and let him pick Mia up and drop her off at the end of the driveway.

But his apology had thrown her off guard, and she just couldn't do it. "I wish I had told you about Mia."

"I do, too."

"I just…I was so afraid you'd take her—or him—away from me when we got divorced. And we would have divorced eventually. And—to be honest—after living with you I didn't think you'd be a good dad."

She felt his hand tense, but it relaxed again after a second. It was a long moment before he spoke. "Who knows...maybe I wouldn't have, not then. I'm a different person now. I'm older, and maybe just a little bit wiser.

And there's a part of me that's never going to forgive you for what you did. She brought her baby book to dinner one night and looking at those pictures...her first birthday and that one where she wrapped the toilet paper all around her head...I swear to God, Gena, I cried right there in the restaurant. Did she tell you about that?"

A hiccupped sob escaped her and she shook her head. She tried to pull her hand away. This was too hard.

"But—" he held her fingers tightly "—neither of us can change what happened before, and I'm thankful that I have her now. We just need to try to start over with a clean slate and keep ourselves in the present, okay?"

Gena nodded, but the tears wouldn't stop flowing. If only they could have talked like this fifteen years ago, their lives might be so different now.

She was still watching the way his fingertip ran back and forth across her nail, but she heard him sigh. "Which brings us back to the other night."

This time when she pulled her fingers away he let her go. She pulled the sleeve of her light sweatshirt down over hand and wiped her eyes and cheeks.

He was back to looking at the table again. "I've been messed up lately, and being here—doing the family thing—got to my head, I guess."

The door swung open and Mr. Coltrane, one of the businessmen who were her regular guests during the week, looked in. "Gena, I hit a button on the TV remote, and now the cable's messed up."

She smiled, grateful for the distraction, and stood up. "No problem. And I'll call you about Saturday, Travis."

"Gena we need to talk about—"

She paused in the doorway and looked back at him. "I think we said it all that night."

<hr/>

This is a disaster. Gena was so tense she was afraid she would shatter at the slightest touch. Every bite of the Chinese food Travis had ordered tasted like sawdust.

She had offered to cook a meal, but he insisted on not putting her out any more than he had to. Insisted over the telephone, of course. She hadn't seen him since Thursday afternoon.

When Travis had picked up Mia on Thursday evening he had parked in the driveway and honked the horn. That was just fine with Gena. The less she saw of him the easier it was to keep her guard up.

Choking down another bite of her shrimp egg roll, she looked around the table, wishing everybody would eat a little bit faster. She had never had guests at the Inn who made her feel as ill at ease as the Ryans.

David and Barbara Ryan were a classic case of two people who lived together for a long time growing to resemble each other very much. They were tall and athletically built, and having money kept them from quite looking their age. Both had thick, wavy hair and blue eyes, though David's weren't as bright as those of his wife and son.

And granddaughter. Mia resembled Travis's family so much that Gena felt like a trespasser at her own table.

"Don't you worry about having strange men live in your house with Mia?" Barbara asked, not even trying to keeping the scorn out of her voice.

So much for a show of family, she thought, returning her former mother-in-law's acidic smile with one of her own. The woman had actually walked through the door and said, "You can call me Mrs. Ryan."

What did she think she was going to call her? *Mom?*

"Actually, they don't live here, and Mia doesn't socialize with them. Sometimes she's the one who checks them in, or refills the muffin basket, but she doesn't spend time with the guests. Her work is done mostly behind the scenes."

"Mother, I explained to you that they live in a separate part of the house, and the only access to it is through the kitchen."

Gena shot Travis a grateful look, but he wasn't looking at her. As a matter of fact, she couldn't remember him looking her way at all.

It was clear he was avoiding her. Maybe he was still angry about her abrupt end to their discussion the other day. She also considered the possibility he was being extra careful in front of his parents. Mrs. Ryan probably wouldn't appreciate knowing her son was attracted to his ex-wife. Gena bit down on a smile when she imagined how the woman would react to the knowledge he had actually kissed her.

They ate in awkward silence for a few more minutes, and all the while she cursed Travis for forcing her into this. His parents had never liked her and they never would. Mia was a big girl, and this pretense thing was getting a little out of hand.

"So, will I still be able to visit you and Kristen in Boston, Dad?" Mia asked when they were finished eating. "It's a bummer I don't get to go shopping with her and get my dress fitted now that you're not getting married."

The only sound in the room was Barbara's sharp intake of breath. Mia's eyes got round when she realized what was going on, and Gena hoped Travis wouldn't be angry with her for breaking the news before he did.

"What does she mean you're not getting married?" Barbara asked her son in a cold voice.

Travis winked at Mia and gave her a reassuring smile before he turned his full attention to his mother. Somehow he had thought they could get through the evening without her finding out, but he should have known better.

"We've decided we're not ready and we'll wait and see how it goes."

"You've been together for four years and you're not ready? What happened?"

He clenched his jaw and looked to his father for help, but David Ryan had developed a sudden interest in his fortune cookie. "There's a lot going on right now, and we just want a little extra time to sort it out."

"You should have told her about Gena," Barbara said firmly. "That's what this is all about, isn't it?"

"I would really prefer to talk about this another time, Mother. This isn't really the place."

Barbara pinned her former daughter-in-law with a cold look. "Does this have anything to do with you?"

Travis sent up a silent prayer that this not get as ugly as he feared it might. "Mother, this has nothing to do with Gena."

"Well, it's not *that* farfetched a notion. She corrupted you once before, so why not now?"

"Corrupted?" Gena demanded from the end of the table. "I *corrupted* him?"

He watched her face redden and her eyes brighten and dropped his head into his hands. There went another prayer unanswered.

"Mom," he heard Mia whisper. "Please don't."

He looked up and directly into Gena's eyes, expecting to see anger and indignation. Instead there was only pain, and it hurt him to see it.

Whatever she might have done in the past, she didn't deserve his mother's abuse. Gena was a good woman and a great mom. If his mother couldn't see that, it was her loss.

"Mother," he said firmly. "Gena did not corrupt me. And I would remind you that you are a guest in her home, at *your* request.

"When Kristen and I get married is nobody else's business, and it has nothing to do with Gena. You're here to spend some time with Mia, and I'll thank you to leave the past in the past."

His mother tried to stare him down, but he didn't look away. Finally, she blinked and nodded. After breathing a sigh of relief he gave Gena an apologetic smile. It was a mistake. Even with the tension in the room she looked warm and inviting, and he didn't want to look away.

Damn, she's gorgeous tonight. With her hair pulled back and a very light sheen of makeup, her eyes and the perfect bow of her mouth were highlighted.

His gaze went to the small diamond studs in her ears, then followed the graceful curve of her neck down to the diamond pendant that rested in the low V-neck of her sweater. She moved her arm and the shirt shifted, rewarding him with just the tiniest hint of her cleavage.

It was enough to make his mouth go dry. He wished suddenly that his parents and Mia would get an urge for ice cream or something else and leave him alone with Gena.

He wanted to kiss her again. She had responded to his kiss before with a longing that made him wonder what she would do if he *really* kissed her. He wanted to run his fingers down her neck, press his mouth to that sweet spot just below the diamond pendant. Imagining her breasts filling his hands filled him with a painful need, and he shifted in his chair, forcibly reminding himself that his mother and daughter were in the room.

Kristen. I love Kristen, he told himself again. It was becoming something of a mantra. He repeated it constantly in his mind, hoping somehow his body would get the message. What he felt for Gena was just some kind of confused lust, and he'd better remember that.

A tiny shiver tickled Gena's spine, and she tried to pretend she didn't notice how Travis was staring at her—practically devouring her with his gaze. She tried to focus on whatever inane topic Barbara had deemed safe for discussion, but all of her senses were held captive by those brilliant blue eyes. What was he doing?

She frowned in his direction, not looking directly at him, but trying to send him a message. If he was attempting to convince his mother she had nothing to do with postponing his wedding, undressing her with his eyes at the dinner table was not the best way to go about it.

But would I want him to stop if our family wasn't here at the table? No, she didn't think she would—or could. There was no sense in lying to herself. She wasn't exactly putty in his hands, but she knew her desire for him was stronger than her willpower—or her common sense. She just hoped he wouldn't test her resolve and act on the thoughts that were making him look at her that way.

"So where are your parents now, Gena?" David Ryan asked in a sincerely interested voice, and she gave him her full attention.

"They're in Florida. They moved there about a year after I opened the Inn."

With that, the conversation moved smoothly into small talk, with Mia doing most of the talking. Gena served dessert and coffee, and they all breathed a sigh of relief when it was time for the Ryans to leave—all three of them.

ChApTeR SeveN

"She actually said that to you?" Jill said as they walked down Main Street.

Gena nodded at her best friend. "I swear she did. She made it sound like I was letting strange men camp out on Mia's floor."

"I can't believe you didn't throw her out!"

"I couldn't. She's Travis's mother—Mia's grandmother. I have to be nice to her. And I think I did pretty well."

Jill snorted and tossed her blonde ponytail. "Then you must be a saint. I remember old *Babs.* Always had her nose so high up in the air I thought she'd drown every time it rained."

They walked in silence for a while, enjoying the sun and the fresh air. Occasionally they nodded to people they knew, and they stopped to buy juice at the natural food store.

"What's new and exciting in your life?" Gena asked, eager to talk and think about anything but the Ryan family.

Jill rolled her eyes. "This is me, remember? Nothing new and exciting ever happens to me. Let's sit in the park. I want to hear more about Travis Ryan."

"There's nothing to tell," Gena insisted, but it was hard to lie to her best friend. Sometimes it seemed Jill knew her better than she knew herself.

"Spill it, girl."

"I think I'm falling in love with him," she blurted out when they sat on the park's granite benches.

Jill didn't react at all the way she expected her to. She just stared. "Again?"

Gena frowned at her friend. "You don't sound very surprised. And it's not *again*. It's different this time."

"I was just teasing you—having some fun. I didn't realize you were this serious about him." Jill gave her a rare grave look. "He's taken, Gena. He's getting married, remember?"

How could she forget? "But not yet. They postponed the wedding. He said maybe next year."

That got a raised eyebrow. "Did he say why?"

"They have to sort some stuff out—" she paused, rolling the juice bottle between her hands "—and he kissed me."

"What?" Jill gripped her elbow. "He kissed you? What did you do?"

Gena used her thumbnail to pick at the label, peeling it away from the glass in thin sheets. She didn't think confession was as good for the soul as she'd heard. "I kissed him back."

"Wow."

Gena laughed, but there wasn't much humor in it. "That's it? Wow? Where's the sage advice I count on you for?"

"I don't know what to say, other than I'll be here for you when you get your heart broken."

Gena felt a flash of anger directed at her best friend—something that hadn't happened in years. Was it so inconceivable that Travis would fall in love with her and break his engagement? He had kissed her, after all.

But then he had called it a mistake and vowed it would never happen again. Jill was right, and she couldn't deny it. "It's too late. My heart's already breaking."

"You have to stop this," Jill said earnestly. "It's not funny anymore. Not only is this going to tear you apart, but think about what it will do to Mia."

"I think Mia wants us to be together." It was a sorry excuse and she knew it.

"Of course she does, but she's only fifteen. You're an adult and you know that even if he's not getting married this fall, he's still engaged. You can't steal another woman's guy. It's not right, and even if you had him first, that was a long time ago."

"Believe me, I know that. It's just…"

Jill put her arm around Gena. "We've been best friends for as long as I can remember, so it really hurts me to say this. Travis Ryan is not the man for you."

"Travis *is* the man for me. I'm just not the woman for *him*."

"Speak of the devil," Jill whispered and Gena jerked her head up.

Sure enough, Travis was just emerging from the barber shop, and despite her quick and fervent prayers, he spotted them. Instead of simply returning her quick wave he made his way across the street.

She watched his long, sure strides and felt an ache in the small of her back. She knew she was staring—maybe even ogling—but couldn't tear her eyes away from him.

The light breeze ruffled his hair and the sunlight danced across the golden strands. The T-shirt he wore stretched across his chest and shoulders, and she admired the way his jeans hugged his legs. She heard Jill's appreciative sigh and had to agree wholeheartedly.

As he grew nearer to the park he didn't smile, but he didn't look angry. She was thankful for that, at least. After confessing her feelings to Jill she was too vulnerable for a confrontation with him. He did smile a little when he reached them.

"Hi, Gena. I was just going up to the Inn to find you."

Jill gave her a none-too-subtle nudge in the ribs with her elbow. "Travis, this is Jill Delaney. I don't know if you remember her. She was behind us in school."

He shook her hand. "We didn't travel in the same circles, but I do remember you. Aren't you the one who glued all Mrs. Paddock's books closed?"

"Yup, that was me," Jill said proudly. "But, I've got to run. Errands, you know?"

"No, you don't," Gena said, hoping she didn't sound as desperate as she felt. She didn't feel strong enough to talk to Travis alone at the moment.

"Yes, I do." She was already walking away. "See you later."

Gena bit down on what she wanted to say and vowed to have a talk with her best friend later about loyalty. To declare that Travis wasn't the man for her, then purposely leave her alone with him was just plain mean.

"Why were you looking for me?" she asked when Travis had taken a seat on another bench. "Are there more of your relatives who can't wait to see me again?"

"I wanted to apologize for the way my mother behaved," he said, grinning sheepishly at her. "If I'd known she was going to be like that I would have had her meet Mia somewhere else."

"It's okay. I'm sorry Mia spilled the beans about your wedding. She didn't know you hadn't said anything to your mom."

He looked down at his hands, giving Gena an opportunity to get her fill of him. His hair was lightened at the ends by the summer sun, and his tan was deepening as he spent more time outside walking around town. She sighed wistfully, making him look at her again.

"I wasn't entirely honest last night," he said. "And it's probably better that we have this conversation in public, rather than at the Inn."

Uh-oh. What was it with him, anyway? Most men dreaded having serious discussions, but that seemed to be all he wanted to do. "Okay."

"You *are* part of the reason Kristen and I aren't getting married now."

Gena swallowed, and had a hard time doing it. "Because of the...kiss?"

He shrugged and looked down at the grass. "Yes. That's a big part of it. But also because I want to kiss you again. I think about it a lot, actually."

Her heart did a somersault in her chest, and she had to concentrate to keep herself from grinning like a fool. He *did* want to kiss her again, so maybe her dreams weren't so farfetched after all.

He continued in a rush of words. "It's not fair to marry Kristen while I have these...thoughts about you. But I *will* marry her, because I love her—and whatever I feel for you, it's not that. It's just some kind of mixed up attraction—maybe because you're the mother of my child. I don't know."

Gena's hopes deflated like a popped balloon. Her burst of laughter was short and bitter, a poor attempt at disguising the ache his words caused in her belly. "That's certainly flattering."

"I'm not trying to hurt your feelings, Gena. I just think it's better to get it all out in the open now, so we can be done with it."

"What is your obsession with talking everything to death?" she demanded in a raised voice. "It was a kiss, Travis. That's it—nothing more. Forget it and move on."

He looked into her eyes. "I can't forget it. That's the problem."

At any other time in her life that kind of statement probably would have made her jump for joy, but not now—not so soon after Jill had reminded her so adamantly of Travis's unavailability. Not so soon after he had reaffirmed his decision to marry Kristen.

Gena was tempted to get up and walk away. He wouldn't try to stop her because a scuffle in a public place wasn't his style.

"And I'm not talking it to death," he continued. "I've barely managed to get two words out of you about it."

Since he was so determined to be a little black cloud and rain on her sunny day, she leaned back against the tree trunk behind her and waited.

"I'm going to make myself pretty scarce around the Inn from now on," he said. "When I pick up Mia I'll just wait in the driveway, and if we need to talk about something, we can do it over the phone.

"I hate myself for what I'm doing to everybody, especially Kristen. I feel like a jerk, and I'm sick of it. I want to…I want to sleep with you, Gena—but I'm not going to, and that's the bottom line."

Gena didn't know whether to laugh or cry. "You can't break up with me, Travis. We aren't dating."

He looked at her, then shook his head. "You know what I mean. I'm talking about this *thing* that's between us."

"There is no *thing*. And there's not going to be a *thing*. You are getting married—eventually. And whether you believe it or not, I don't really want to hurt Kristen either. She's going to be Mia's stepmother and it's pretty important she and I have a good relationship."

But it's all just logic, Travis thought. And logic was having no effect on the confusion and guilt he had been wrapped up in since seeing Gena again for the first time.

He had tried telling himself that it was only because his intimate relationship with Kristen had been in a slump recently. He even tried convincing himself wanting to make love to Gena was some sort of attempt on the part of his subconscious to be a *real* family for Mia. He had tried everything.

"You've been with Kristen for a long time," Gena said softly. "Do you love her?"

"Yes," Travis said quickly, not letting himself stop to wonder if it was true—if he was still *in* love with her.

"Then you need to remember that. Physical attraction comes and goes, but if you love a woman and she loves you, then you should try not to screw it up."

She was right. So why did it hurt so much to hear her say it? "So, I…I'll try not to bump into you too much then."

"Good," she said firmly. "I've got to run now, but give me a call when you want to see Mia."

He said goodbye, but she was already walking away. But she hadn't turned fast enough to keep him from seeing the tears in her eyes.

Two weeks later, Travis sat in the emergency room waiting area, fuming and wondering where his plan had gone wrong.

It had seemed so simple at the time—stay away from Gena Taylor. If he wasn't alone with her he wouldn't be tempted to touch her—to kiss her again. With a little distance between them he would see he'd felt nothing for her but a passing physical attraction.

But he neglected to factor Mia into the equation. Their daughter seemed determined to throw her parents together at every opportunity and he was finally starting to realize she was doing it deliberately.

She had arranged for each of them to pick her up at the mall, then she was in the bathroom for fifteen minutes—leaving Travis and Gena to *talk*. She had pleaded for another movie night until they gave in, but this time he was careful to get the rocking chair before the scheming teenager did. It had been awkward—knowing they were both remembering the last movie night—but they survived without incident.

She talked her mom into going for a walk, and they just happened to be in front of Smitty's when he left the restaurant. At first he thought it was a coincidence, but then he remembered telling her that on the days he was in New Hampshire he had breakfast there at eight o'clock every morning. They had to figure out a way to stop her. Not only was it unhealthy for Mia to continue hoping for something that wasn't going to happen, but it was hell on him, too.

He also found spending as little time as possible with Gena wasn't lessening his desire for her. Instead it had grown into a throbbing ache that flared whenever he saw her, and short of becoming an alcoholic, he saw no cure in sight.

It had occurred to him very late one night that he should just go for it. He should end his relationship with Kristen and see where things ended up with Gena. Maybe whatever chemistry they had between them was real.

He rubbed his hands over his face and reminded himself yet again why it couldn't happen. The little girl who was so intent on throwing them together would be surprised to know that she was one of the biggest reasons they couldn't be.

Mia hadn't had to deal with the pain and confusion of their divorce because she wasn't born yet. She just had a mom and a dad. There were no memories of a happy family for her to mourn, and there was no nasty breakup to remember. She wanted them to be together so her family would be complete, but she had no idea how much it could hurt if it went wrong.

What if he and Gena were just feeling a case of good, old-fashioned lust? Mia would be devastated if the relationship didn't work out and she had to suffer through the inevitable ending. They had managed to put their feelings about the past into the background, concentrating on what Mia needed now. But with a breakup would come a whole new round of animosity, accusations, and anger.

He may not have been a dad for long, but he knew his job was to do whatever was best for his daughter. And if that meant exercising more control over his feelings that he thought possible, so be it.

Gena walked back into the waiting room and sank into a chair across from Travis. "I'm sorry she did this. *Again.*"

She promised herself she would have a nice long chat with her daughter when they got home. Even though she couldn't prove it, she knew Mia's ankle injury was fake. The doctor said it was possible she had just twisted it wrong and the pain was already fading, but Gena knew exactly what game she was playing.

"Don't worry about it," Travis said. "I'm just glad she's okay."

"Of course she's okay. She was never hurt. And she's grounded for the rest of her life."

"I think what she's doing is pretty normal under the circumstances," he argued. "Remember—the teen mind is my specialty."

Gena laughed. "Yes, but this is your daughter and that makes it different."

"We should talk to her about what she's doing and give her a warning before grounding her, although I have to admit she scared me to death. I've never gotten a call from the emergency room before."

"It's no fun. I've been called twice from school before, but nothing horrible, thank goodness. A bumped head one time, and two stitches in her knee the other."

He felt a pang of regret for not knowing that. "Are we almost done here?"

"She's done with the doctor. As soon as she gets out of the ladies' room we can leave."

"She does spend a lot of time in the bathroom."

"Maybe I should put her back in diapers," Gena muttered.

Travis laughed and she realized how much she had missed that sound. "Does she really think we'll rekindle some fantasy romance in the time she takes in the bathroom?"

"That's why she spends at least ten or fifteen minutes in there." She chewed on her bottom lip for a few seconds, then asked, "How's Kristen?"

He leaned forward and started rearranging the magazines on the table in front of him. "She's good. We've done a lot of talking and we'll be okay."

Gena had to fight hard for the smile, but she managed. "That's great. I'm happy for you."

Liar, she sang in her mind. A part of her wondered if the reason she hadn't put a stop to Mia's little game already was the fact that she would take almost any excuse to see her ex-husband.

Sometimes when she was tossing and turning in bed she would imagine the life they could have together. She could picture their wedding—a small and intimate affair at the Inn with Mia standing beside them. Then their daughter would go to a friend's house while she and Travis spent their wedding night in bed.

But it wasn't going to happen. Kristen wasn't going away and Travis was no less determined to see his relationship with her work.

"Mia will be starting school soon," Travis continued. "I'm going to keep this schedule for a few more weeks. But I'll be spending more time in Boston again after that. We'll need to work out the weekend and holiday thing. I'll come up to watch her cheer when I can, and for her piano recitals."

She had known it was coming, but it didn't soften the blow. He wasn't going to be a casual part of their lives anymore. There would be weekend visitations, holiday scheduling, arguments over who got her for Christmas.

"It'll work out," she said quietly. "We're only three hours away from each other, so it's not as if everything has to be written in stone."

"There's something else. We're thinking about going to Mexico in the spring and we'd like to take Mia with us." He paused and looked up at her. "There's a possibility we'll get married in Mexico and skip the whole big wedding thing. But we want Mia to be with us."

And there it was. The wedding was going to take place and Travis and Kristen would live happily ever after. She was surprised it even hurt anymore. She couldn't be sure any words coming out of her mouth would be congratulatory, so she simply nodded.

She knew he didn't expect her to say anything. He was a smart man and he dealt with emotions for a living. She could see in his face he knew he was walking all over her heart. At least he looked sorry for it.

"I'm ready, guys," Mia said from the doorway, and as they walked to the parking lot, Gena noticed she forgot to limp.

She waited until she was alone with her daughter and on the road home before she turned off the radio and glanced over at Mia. "Why did you call both of us?"

"I got the answering machine and I didn't know where you were or when you would be home, so I called Dad. I guess you got the message and came too."

"I ran to the store for milk. Why didn't you call my cell phone?"

Mia shrugged, staring out her side window. "I forgot the number."

"Don't lie to me, Mia Dawn Taylor," Gena hissed, making her daughter's head whip around. "You have known that number since the day I got the phone. I want you to stop this little game you're playing right now."

"What game?" Mia looked angry, but Gena knew her well enough to see the stubborn determination not to get caught. "I was hurt and needed a parent. You weren't home, so I called Dad. What's the big deal?"

"The big deal is that you weren't hurt to begin with. You keep trying to throw Travis and I together and you need to stop."

Mia sniffed and turned back to her window. "Believe whatever you want, Mom."

A little bit of doubt undermined Gena's conviction that Mia was guilty. It was possible she wasn't doing it purposely, and there had to be many times other divorced parents bumped into each other. They shared a child, after all.

But not for a second did she buy the excuse that Mia had forgotten her cell phone number. "You can thank your father for the fact that you're not grounded right now."

That got her attention. "Grounded for what? For hurting my ankle?"

"For…you know what for." Gena knew she couldn't win this conversation. There wasn't any way to prove Mia hadn't hurt her ankle, or even that she hadn't forgotten the number.

She hoped the knowledge that her mother suspected her might be enough to put a halt to Mia's schemes, so she changed the subject. "Are you going to your dad's tonight?"

"Yes," Mia said in an *I'm not talking to you* voice.

Let her sulk, Gena thought. It was her own fault. "I thought you were. I'm going out tonight, so Donna will be at the house."

"Where are you going?" Mia asked with a little more interest.

"To the gallery. The exhibit of Mr. Schofield's work opens tonight."

"Oh." Mia slouched down in her seat. "Stained glass—how exciting."

Gena stuck her tongue out at her daughter. "I like stained glass. Should I write my cell phone number on the back of your hand?"

"Very funny. It's on Dad's speed dial. I put both numbers on it, so he can always reach us. Your cell is number two."

"That's great," Gena muttered. It didn't surprise her any. Where Travis was concerned, she always came in second.

Chapter Eight

Travis opened the door, surprised to find Mia standing there. "Hey, kiddo. I forgot you were coming over tonight."

There was still a trace of shyness about her he knew only time would erase. "Is it okay?"

"Sure." He stepped back and let her into the small suite. "I'm going out pretty soon, but—"

"Can I stay and play with the laptop?" she interrupted.

He laughed and waved his hand at the desk where it sat. "Help yourself. You can borrow it for the night if you just want to take it home."

She thought about it, then shook her head. "I shouldn't. Mom would kill me if something happened to it and she had to replace it."

There was always a little sadness whenever he saw Mia—regret for the lost years—but now it swelled up again. "She wouldn't have to replace it, Mia. I'm your father and if you break my laptop I will take care of it."

She smiled at him, her big blue eyes reflecting his own. "Sorry. I know…it's just…I've never had a dad before, so it's always Mom—Mom—Mom."

"I know. But it's okay. I've never had a daughter before, so we're even."

She grinned and flipped up the screen on the small computer. "Where are you going, anyway?"

He sighed and pulled a sour face at her. "That little gallery downtown. A guy I knew in high school does stained glass and I couldn't think of a good reason not to go see it."

"Oh—" she rolled her eyes "Mr. Schofield."

"That's the one. Are you sure you'll be okay here by yourself?"

"Yes, Dad," she said with an impish grin. "I won't open the door and take candy from strangers."

"Very funny." He took a deep breath, searching for the right way to phrase the question he had to ask. "Did your mom talk to you about…did she have a talk with you after you left the hospital?"

Mia rolled her eyes. "Yes. I wasn't doing it on purpose, you know. But I'll try not to do whatever it is you guys think I'm doing."

Not for a second did he think she was telling the truth. Those blue eyes were just a little too wide with innocence, and the corners of her mouth turned up a bit too serenely. But Gena had talked to her about it, so he hoped that would take care of it.

"You're not going to wear that, are you?" Mia asked, but the scowl she directed at his jeans and T-shirt didn't quite correspond with the gleam in her eye.

"Why not? It's an art exhibit, not a fashion show."

"You should still look nice." She gave him a smile that should have set off warning bells and walked to his closet. "Let's see what else you've got."

The small gallery was nearly filled to capacity. Travis looked around while he hung his coat on the rack near the door. He remembered some of the guests from high school, but most were strangers to him.

He hated occasions like these and Kristen usually had to drag him along kicking and screaming if she wanted to see an exhibit. But Paul Schofield had been one of his teammates in high school, so when he ran into him at the store he hadn't been able to turn down the invitation. Paul was an insurance salesman by day, but his passion was stained glass, and Travis had agreed to come, in part just to shut him up.

He saw Paul across the room and waved, then starting making his way through the crowd. Somebody pressed a sheet of paper into his hand and he looked down at the program which listed Paul's name and the titles of his pieces. *Dandelions in Sunlight...Tulip Tapestry?*

Shannon Stacey

Not exactly what he expected from a guy who'd been the best linebacker in their division, but he smiled and shook Paul's hand. "Great show."

The other man's face glowed with pride and excitement. "This is a pretty good turnout. It doesn't hurt that in this town there's nothing else to do on a weekday night, but still...I'm happy with it."

"I like the...um—roses," Travis said, pointing to a large pane of glass which stood on a table near them.

Paul shrugged. "Flowers are good sellers. This one's a smaller version of the one I did for the front door of the Riverside Inn."

Gena's house, he thought. Everywhere he turned she seemed to be there in one way or another. So many things reminded him of her—a hint of her perfume on a woman he passed by at the bank, an antique creamer he knew she would like that he spied in the window display at the secondhand shop.

"I'm glad you came," Paul continued. "You could have knocked me over with a feather when I heard you were back in town. And the whole thing with Gena...wow."

Travis tried to give him a silencing glare, but the man was looking around the gallery and missed it. "When I heard down at the hardware store you were the Taylor girl's father, I thought to myself *no way.* I mean—you and Gena Taylor—not in a million years.

"Then I heard it somewhere else, too, and from somebody who would know. Couldn't believe it. I thought you were dating that hot chick...what was her name?"

"I don't remember," he replied coldly.

He did remember, but the last thing he wanted to do was walk down memory lane again with Paul. He had been doing enough of that on his own.

"She's here somewhere," Paul said. "Gena, I mean."

She's here? He scanned the crowd again, looking for a glimmer of auburn hair. It had only been earlier that day that he told her—and reminded himself—that he was getting married in the spring, and he hated the rush of excitement he felt now. If he knew what was good for him he would just walk out the door.

Paul said he was off to mingle and Travis muttered something appropriate as he left, but he was intent on finding Gena. He couldn't say why—they had nothing to say to each other. He just wanted to see her.

Finally his gaze locked onto her and he drew a deep breath. She was with Jill Delaney and another woman who looked vaguely familiar, but whose name he couldn't recall.

Gena wore a short, dark green sundress with a cream sweater, and even though she faced slightly away from him, he could see from her expression she was having a great time. With her hair freed from its usual braid and swinging around her shoulders she took his breath away.

He watched her laugh at something Jill said and his stomach tightened. From where he was standing he couldn't hear her, but he could see she was relaxed—having fun.

She was never like that with him. There was always tension—usually anger, guilt or blame. He hated the shadows he always saw in her eyes and the way her lips thinned whenever he had to say something that would hurt her.

A woman passed with a tray of drinks and he took one with a smile of thanks. He took a sip—grimacing at the tart white grape juice—without ever taking his eyes off Gena.

"Don't look to your left, but he's watching you," Jill whispered.

Gena turned and met his luminous blue gaze, which even from this distance radiated heat. She gave him a quick, impersonal smile, then turned back to Jill before he could react.

What is he doing here? Her pulse quickened, but she forced herself to look casual. This was the last place she had expected to run into him, and she wasn't sure she wanted to see him.

The conversation they had in the emergency room was still too fresh in her mind. Travis was getting married in the spring, so what had passed between them meant nothing to him. She could pretend it meant as little to her, but it wasn't easy.

"I told you not to look," Jill muttered.

She laughed, although it sounded a little forced even to her own ears. "You sound like a kid."

"Well, you're acting like one."

Gena took another glass of juice from Paul's wife as she passed by with the tray. "I am not. And if you say *are too*—I'm leaving."

Jill's eyes grew wide and Gena resisted the urge to look over her shoulder. "Tell me he's not coming over here. He's not, is he?"

"He sure is."

She squeezed the glass in her hand, trying to remain calm. She couldn't imagine what he wanted with her, but at least he would behave himself in public. He had lived in the town long enough to know gossip was the number one pastime.

She waited until she could sense his presence behind her before she turned. "Hello, Travis."

"Hi. I...umm...I just wanted you to know Mia was playing that game of hers when I left. When I told her I was going out she asked if she could stay, and I didn't see why not."

Gena nodded, but she sensed they were both aware she already knew that. Mia had fallen in love with her father's laptop, which was much faster than their ancient machine, and spent every free moment she could playing with it. So why come over here to tell her?

"I thought so," she said. "And I knew she was going over—that's why I got Donna to watch the desk tonight. I didn't know you were coming here, though."

"I ran into Paul earlier and he invited me."

The silence grew awkward then and Gena was grateful when Jill pulled her sister forward. "Travis, this is my sister, Liz. She graduated a year before you guys did."

"Liz—" he shook her hand "—how are you?"

"Good. My husband's watching the kids and I'm here. What could be better?"

"School starts next week," Gena offered.

Liz lifted her glass. "Thank goodness."

They all laughed, but Gena was keenly aware of Travis standing beside her. What was he doing...and why? Them being in the same place at the same time was bound to happen, even without Mia's help, but there was no reason for him to seek her out of the crowd.

Travis Ryan was the master of mixed messages, she decided. On the one hand he sought her out, touched her, kissed her...wanted her.

But on the other hand, he was constantly pushing her away. He reminded her—and himself, no doubt—that he was engaged to another woman every chance he got. He had made it clear that his interest in her would never come to anything.

She just wasn't sure if he meant it. Sometimes the words coming out of his mouth didn't coincide with the heat—and the need—in his eyes. Some of his more devastating words echoed in her mind.

I didn't want you... I'll never forgive you... A mistake I won't make again... I want to sleep with you, Gena, but I'm not going to...

Yet here he was. Not only in the gallery, but at her elbow, laughing with her friends. Of all the people in the crowd, why did he choose her to mingle with?

To say hello, dummy, she scolded herself. They were acquaintances at the least, weren't they? He stopped to say hi and he would no doubt move off into the crowd again as soon as Liz stopped jabbering about shopping for school clothes.

Over Jill's shoulder she could see another man approaching their small group and she groaned inwardly. Joe Kirkwood had been working himself up to ask her out for about three years. She prayed this wouldn't be the occasion at which he found the courage.

He was nice enough guy and he really liked Mia, but she had never thought they had the chemistry for a romantic relationship. Now that Travis had reappeared, making her heart pound and her toes curl, she was sure of it.

"Hi Gena," he said and he nodded to Jill and Liz. She watched him look Travis over, and his smile soured just a little.

"Joe, this is Travis Ryan. Maybe you remember him from school?"

He nodded and extended his hand. "Good to see you again, Travis."

Travis shook the man's hand, subtly increasing the pressure on his knuckles until Joe winced. Maybe it was ridiculous to feel jealousy over a woman he wasn't willing to claim as his own, but the way Kirkwood had looked at Gena turned his stomach.

Unwelcome images of her in this man's arms clouded his mind, but he had the foresight to let go of Joe's hand before he did serious damage to it. "Nice to see you, too."

He didn't need to see Gena's furrowed brow or the rolling of her eyes to know there hadn't been a drop of sincerity in his voice. He didn't care. There was no way he was going to let this guy into Gena's life. Or if he was already in it—he was on his way out.

The level of his anger at Joe Kirkwood made Travis a little uneasy. He spent too much time telling himself what he felt for Gena wasn't serious to care if she was interested in this guy. He just couldn't seem to tamp down the dark jealousy that clouded his mind.

I'm Mia's father, he told himself. Of course he had a right to approve or disapprove of any man who could end up as her stepfather. And he definitely didn't approve of Joe Kirkwood. He didn't like the hunger in the man's eyes when he looked at Gena.

"You should have told me you were coming," Joe said to her. "I would have given you a ride."

"I walked actually, but maybe next time."

The nagging jealousy exploded in Travis's brain and without thinking he laid a possessive hand on the small of Gena's back.

Gena froze, hardly able to believe the heat suddenly radiating from her back was Travis's hand. *How dare he?*

She noted the stunned expressions on the faces of her friends, then the resentment and disappointment that darkened Joe's. She tried to make a subtle movement away from Travis, but he moved with her. Short of making a scene, there was nothing she could do about it.

Joe made a show of looking over her shoulder. "I...uh...I see somebody over there I need to talk to. I'll see you later."

He moved off into the crowd and Gena tilted her face up to glare at Travis. What kind of game was he playing now? He didn't want her, but nobody else could have her?

His hand fell away from her waist, and Gena felt relief and a sense of loss in equal measure. "What do you think you're doing?"

She watched him glance at Jill and Liz, then shrug. Her hands trembled from the riot of emotions she was feeling—anger, desire, embarrassment, hurt— and she gripped the glass she held very tightly. She wanted to fling the contents in Travis's face, but she managed to rein in her temper.

She looked up at him again. His jaw was clenched and she got the sense he was as upset about what had just happened as she was.

Good, she fumed. And she hoped he realized the entire town would spend days speculating about their relationship. Even worse than that would be her own speculation. *A master of mixed messages,* she thought again.

Well, she wasn't going to be his emotional punching bag anymore. If he didn't want her—totally and without reservation—then he could take a hike.

Without saying a word, she turned and walked away. She heard him call her name once, but she didn't stop. If he came after her, she had no idea what she would do, so she didn't even look over her shoulder.

It seemed to take forever to make her way through the crowd to the bathroom, but she breathed a deep sigh of relief when she locked herself into the stall.

She spent a few minutes sitting on the closed lid, trying to bolster her resolve. She wasn't sure how much good it would do. She just didn't seem to be able to master the one skill that might protect her heart—pretended indifference. If she could manage that, she could keep Travis at bay.

If she could convince him she didn't want him, she would be one step closer to convincing herself. If it was even possible. Keeping her distance was probably a good place to start, but she couldn't hide in the bathroom forever.

All she could do was turn a cold shoulder to him. Travis didn't need to see the pain he inflicted—didn't need to see she still craved his touch in spite of it. She was done wearing her heart on her sleeve.

Before leaving the sanctuary of the restroom she stopped in front of the mirror and looked herself in the eye. "Indifference," she whispered.

It didn't matter. When she stepped out into the crowd, she couldn't stop herself from looking for him. Travis was already gone.

The next evening Travis entered his hotel room to find the phone ringing. He dropped his keys on the table and snatched up the receiver. "Hello?"

"Hello, Travis."

Kristen. The disappointment he felt upon not hearing Gena's voice on the other end of the line filled him with guilt.

He had left before she returned from the restroom to avoid having to explain why he had so stupidly put his hand on her back. It was an overtly possessive gesture, practically screaming to everybody that she belonged to him.

"Travis?"

He wrenched his thoughts back to his fiancée. "Kristen, honey, it's so good to hear your voice."

"You'd hear it more often if you returned my calls."

He hesitated, trying to recall if the hotel manager had left any message slips lying around. "When did you call?"

"Last night. I called twice and Mia answered both times."

Damn that girl. "She didn't tell me you called, honey. If she had I would have called you back as soon as I got in."

There was silence on the other end and Travis knew something was wrong. Something more than not having her phone calls returned. "Kristen?"

"Where were you?" she asked, and he wasn't sure, but it sounded like she might be crying.

"There's an art gallery downtown that features local artists and craftsmen. A guy I went to school with was holding an exhibit. I ran into him and he invited me, so I went down for a while."

"With Gena."

Travis felt the hair on the back of his arms tingle. What had Mia told her? "Gena was there, yes. She lets artists display their work at the Inn sometimes, and she always goes to the openings."

"Mia told me 'Dad's at the gallery with Mom'."

He closed his eyes and sighed. They should have nipped Mia's plans in the bud a long time ago. "We were there at the same time, but not together. She was with a group of friends. We said hello, and that was all. I wasn't there very long, but I stopped and grabbed some takeout on the way home. I only saw her for a few minutes."

Just long enough to make an ass of myself, he thought, but chose not to say aloud. He pictured the look Gena had given him before she walked away, and the ache in his chest that had become his constant companion worsened. *How could I do something so stupid?*

Kristen was silent, so he tried to think of something else to say. "Mia was here because there's some game she likes to play on my laptop because her computer is too slow. There's nothing else to it, Kristen."

"Mia says you spend a lot of time together." Her voice was icy now, any trace of tears gone.

He swore, and then explained as best he could what Mia had been up to. He couldn't admit that he never really tried to stop her. He didn't want it to stop. Seeing Gena was always on his mind, even if it was just for a few minutes.

"Are you in love with Gena?" she asked when he was finished talking.

Travis hesitated—he wasn't sure he knew anymore—then said simply, "No."

He sensed immediately he had waited too long. He expected her to lash out at him or to slam down the phone, but she did nothing for a long few seconds. She didn't sound like she was crying—she just waited.

"I don't know what I feel...about anything," he said finally. "I promise you we were not at the gallery *together*. The only time we see each other is when Mia pulls her little stunts."

"Did you tell them we aren't getting married?" she asked after a long silence.

He tried to think, tried to understand why it mattered. "Umm...I told them we aren't getting married this fall. I told Gena we might get married in Mexico, but I'm not sure if I told Mia."

As soon as the words left his mouth he realized what he'd admitted. "We were at the emergency room, Kristen. I was just trying to make small talk. I don't spend time alone with Gena except during Mia's damned trips to the bathroom."

"She made it pretty clear you and her mother are...an item. She was *surprised* I called because she thought we were over."

Travis felt a surge of anger at his daughter. No matter what childish games she might play with her parents, she had no right to deliberately hurt Kristen.

"She's fifteen and she thinks she wants us to be together. She'll get over it in time, sweetheart."

"I don't have time in my life for these kinds of games, Travis. I—"

For a second he thought she would end it. She would tell him their relationship was over and he was free to do whatever he wanted.

He wasn't sure he would be sorry. Even though he couldn't take the chance of becoming romantically involved with Gena—for Mia's sake—he was being disloyal to Kristen. It was only in his mind, but he didn't like the feeling.

"I can wait a little bit longer, Travis, because I love you and I know you're going through a big emotional upheaval. But you need to figure it out soon."

He heard the click as she hung up the phone and he stared at the receiver while his anger built. It was time to have that little talk with Mia.

Chapter Nine

Gena knew Travis was angry the second she opened the door. His jaw was tight and there wasn't even a hint of warmth in his eyes. *What did I do now?* she thought.

"Where's Mia?"

His clipped words set off her inner alarm bells. "She's watching TV. Why, what's the—"

He pushed by her and went through the kitchen and into their living room, Gena following on his heels. "Travis, what are you doing?"

She saw Mia look up, and noted the way her chin came up and how she caught her bottom lip between her teeth. It was a look she'd seen many times. Her daughter had done something very wrong and knew she had been caught.

"Why did you lie to Kristen?" he demanded harshly, and Gena winced at his tone.

"I didn't lie. You *were* at the gallery with Mom."

Gena moved around Travis so she could see his face. "What's going on?"

He looked down at her, then back at Mia. "Our daughter told my fiancée that we were at the gallery together, then mentioned her *surprise* that she and I were still planning on getting married."

He pointed his finger at the girl. "And even if you didn't technically lie you went out of your way to make it look as if there's something going on between your mother and I."

Mia smirked. "There is, isn't there?"

Gena froze, knowing she should step in, but unable to think of a single thing to say. She hoped Travis would. Mia was only fifteen— they couldn't tell her the truth, whatever that was. Looking her in the face and outright lying didn't seem the right thing to do either.

"There is nothing going on between us," Travis said in a low voice. "There's not going to be either, despite the little games you've been playing."

Well, that answers that, Gena thought, feeling a pang of hurt and regret. He'd sent the message loud and clear, and she got it.

"And furthermore," he continued, "My relationships with *anybody* but you are none of your business. Kristen has been nothing but nice to you, and what you did was just plain mean."

Mia tightened her lips, but she couldn't hide the quivering. "I'm sorry. I didn't mean for it to come out like that. She must have misunderstood me."

"There's no misunderstanding," Travis replied. "You have been trying to get your mother and I together from the beginning. I guess you thought that would be easier with Kristen out of the picture."

Mia didn't need to respond to the accusation. Although she kept her face lowered, Gena could see the guilty flush on her cheeks. And even though it was her own fault, Gena felt a spark of pity. So far Travis had been the laid-back, fun loving parent, and this couldn't be easy for either of them.

"Now, I'm going to say this once and for all—" he pointed at Mia "—it is *not* going to happen."

Embarrassment made Gena's face feel hot and she clenched her hands into fists. Being rejected was bad enough—having it happen in front of her daughter was downright humiliating.

Travis folded his arms across his chest. "And I think you should be grounded, young lady—including piano."

"But my recital—"

"You heard me."

There was a moment of stunned silence, then Gena moved to stand between Travis and Mia. "Now, hold on just a minute. I think that's a little harsh."

"Is she my daughter?" He demanded in a shout that Gena hoped any guests milling around hadn't heard.

"Yes, but—"

"Then I will punish her as I see fit."

Fury poured like lava through her veins, fueled by her lingering humiliation. "Who the hell do you think you are? Mia lives in *my* house, she obeys *my* rules, and *I* will punish her."

"I am her parent too, and it's my life she's messing with," he yelled back. "And she might have been living under *my* roof if you hadn't kept her from me."

"That has nothing to do with this."

"Mom, it's okay," Mia said, clearly hoping to placate her father.

"No. It is not okay." She pointed her finger at Travis. "You can't just waltz in here and start giving orders. And *I* pay for her piano lessons. I pay a lot for them, in fact, and she *will* play."

"I have the right to discipline my daughter," Travis insisted in a cold voice. "Unless…maybe the reason you don't want her punished is because you put her up to it—or at least encouraged it."

Gena felt the cold wash over her, and she sucked in her breath. "What did you just say?"

"You heard me."

Gena exhaled slowly, then turned to her daughter. "Mia, I want you to go upstairs for a few minutes."

"Mom, I—"

"Just go!"

Gena waited until she heard Mia's door slam closed, followed by the blast of her stereo, before she faced Travis again.

"How dare you accuse me of using my daughter to break up your relationship?"

He didn't back down from her heated glare. "Did you?"

"For goodness sake, this isn't a soap opera or some sleazy talk show. I'll admit not telling you about Mia is the biggest mistake I've ever made, but that doesn't give you the right to drag my entire character down into the mud."

Travis sighed and plunged his hands into his hair as he started to pace. "Fine, so you didn't put her up to it. It just really ticks me off that you won't let me punish her. What she did was wrong, and I'm her father, dammit."

"I didn't say you couldn't punish her. I said you were being a little too harsh."

"Maybe you wouldn't think so if you had just spoken to Kristen."

"And what she did was pretty typical of her age and situation, I think. You said so yourself. Maybe you should have started a little smaller, like no computer or no phone—no sleepovers."

"And I might lose the woman I..."

Gena held her breath, waiting for him to finish. The woman he what? *Loves?*

"—the woman I'm going to marry," he said finally.

Gena stared down at the floor so he couldn't see her face. "She loves playing the piano. She looks forward to her recitals and there's nothing worse you could do to punish her. She'll hate you."

"She'll get over it."

"Maybe not. Soon you're going to be seeing her a lot less, and then what? You'll miss a recital, you'll be busy a couple of weekends, and before you know it this great summer you guys have had will be ancient history."

"No," he said fiercely. "I'm not going to be one of those absentee dads. And that's why I think it's so important you respect me when I try to discipline her."

"I do. I also know you don't have a lot of experience with teenage daughters and you just jumped in the deep end. I was trying to help."

Travis threw up his hands and walked toward the door. "This is ridiculous. We'll talk later when everybody's had a chance to calm down."

"You can't just walk out on this," Gena said, following him into the kitchen. "We need to decide what we're going to do. It's not fair to just leave her wondering."

"What she did to Kristen wasn't fair, either."

Gena couldn't argue with that, so she was silent, waiting for him to make up his mind. Was he leaving or staying?

Travis leaned his head back against the doorjamb, wondering—not for the first time—how he had ended up in this situation. His anger was fading, and he had to admit that Gena knew a lot more about teenage girls than he did.

Most of his clients were teenagers, but they were primarily boys, and they talked mostly about sports. The proper punishment for trying to chase off a father's fiancée had never come up.

The idea of Mia hating him wasn't something he even wanted to consider. Not that he was always going to be the good guy, but he'd like to get to know her better before he started alienating her.

"Do you really think I'll do that—" he looked over at Gena, "—become an absentee dad?"

He saw her hesitate, and he didn't like it.

"I think there's going to be a lot of times when Mia's going to take a back seat," she said.

His anger resumed its slow burn, and he crossed his arms. "What makes you say that?"

"Right now this situation works for you. But after you and Kristen get married she might not be thrilled about having a teenaged stepdaughter. And then you might have..."

He watched her draw a deep breath before she continued. "You might have babies with Kristen and you won't be able to keep running up here."

Babies? An image of Gena pregnant filled his mind. He'd left before she started showing, but he could imagine her heavy with his child, her face round and glowing. He could see himself pressing his face to her stomach, talking to the little person they had created together.

But she was the wrong woman. He shook his head slightly, then tried to refocus on what Gena had said. "I won't ever abandon Mia. Not for Kristen, not for other children, not for anybody."

Gena felt the bitter taste of sorrow in the back of her throat. He wouldn't abandon Mia and she knew that. But he was going to abandon her.

She had reminded herself of that fact so many times she'd lost count, but it didn't lessen the hurt. If anything, the pain flourished, taking root in the deepest recesses of her heart.

Loving Travis Ryan would always be an open wound. Maybe if he disappeared totally from her life she could heal, but she would have to see him—and his wife—for a very long time. He wasn't going to stop being Mia's father.

She cursed the tears that gathered in her eyes, blurring her view of Travis as he moved closer to her.

He touched her arm, hesitantly. "Hey, what's the matter?"

"Nothing."

"Then why are you crying?" He peered down into her face and Gena turned her head away.

"I'm not crying. I just…"

He took her chin and tilted her face up to his. "You just what?"

She couldn't remember—couldn't even think with his face so close to hers. Their breath mingled between them, and she closed her eyes as his lips lowered ever closer to hers.

"Travis?" she whispered.

Travis didn't even try to stop himself—he didn't think he could even if he wanted to. He was already lost.

Anger at his own weakness fueled his desire, making him grip her arms tightly and bring his mouth down on hers with punishing force.

She gasped against his lips and he reveled in the sound, wanting her to be shocked—to push him away. Instead he felt her fingers slide up his neck and into his hair, holding him to her.

His tongue parted her lips, not to rouse her passion, but to demand it. He bit gently at her lower lip, and when she pressed her body to his, he increased the pressure.

She moaned and he felt the bite of her fingernails on his back. The desire that flared in his body shook him, weakened his knees, and he pulled back just a little.

"I can't kiss you—" he ran his hands up either side of her face, his thumbs pressing into her flesh "—and I can't *not* kiss you."

He kissed her again, hard. "You're driving me insane," he muttered against her lips.

Gena opened her eyes, staring into his luminous blue gaze. She saw the torture—the need—and knew they mirrored her own.

One of his hands gripped her hair again, pulling her mouth to his, while the other slid over her back and to her hip, pulling her hard up against him.

A searing hunger she had never felt before took her breath away, and she surrendered to his ravishment of her mouth. Every place his lips pressed—every place his fingertips caressed—seemed to burn even hotter than the rest of her flushed skin.

He shifted his body, pressing his thigh high between her legs, and she groaned against his mouth. His lips left hers, and she waited for them to blaze a new molten trail, at her ear—down her neck.

The kisses didn't come. When she opened her eyes the flames of passion turned to shards of ice.

He looked dismayed...appalled. She winced when he cursed and slapped the wall next to them. She touched his shoulder, silently questioning, but he shrugged her off.

"I can't do this," he said in an anguished voice. "Why do you do this to me?"

She stared at him, her chest rising and falling rapidly as her breathless desire became rage. "You kissed me."

He turned away and kicked one of the kitchen chairs. "I can't hurt Kristen like this."

The emotional rollercoaster was too much for Gena and she felt her control start to slip. "Kristen. You can't hurt *Kristen*?"

She could hear the hysterical note creeping into her voice and she didn't care. "You don't want to hurt Kristen, and you don't want to hurt Mia. How come you have never once cared if you hurt *me*?"

He looked confused and she got the impression he'd never really thought about it. That infuriated her. She wanted to scream at him—to rant and rave—but she remembered in time that Mia was upstairs. This was a conversation she didn't need to overhear.

"What do you want me to do?" he shouted, obviously not having the same consideration.

"I want you stop playing games. If you're going to marry Kristen—fine, just stop kissing me. And if you're not going to marry her, then you need to tell her."

Gena waited for what seemed like an eternity for him to say something...anything.

"I don't know *what* I'm doing," he finally said in a low voice. "Is that what you want to hear?"

She refused to let herself feel pity for him. "Well you need to figure it out because I'm not going to play this game with you anymore."

He tried to touch her arm, but she moved away. "If you ever try to touch me again, Travis Ryan, I swear to God I'll break your fingers."

He recoiled from her anger and she felt a jolt of satisfaction. "And do you know what's kind of funny?"

He frowned and started pacing again. "None of this is funny."

"Ironic, then. Of the three women in your life right now, I seem to be the only one you don't care about hurting—"

"That's—"

"—and *I'm* the one who has loved you the longest."

She turned and walked out before he could form a reply. A second later Travis heard the bathroom door slam closed.

He stood motionless. He should go after her. He couldn't just walk out the door and leave her this upset. He started to swing the door open, then stopped.

What would he say to her? He didn't think he could tell her what she wanted to hear. He knew he couldn't, because all he could offer her now were empty words of comfort.

I'm the one who has loved you the longest.

The words seared across his heart as they echoed through his mind. Never once—not since they met on that first day of kindergarten—had he given her any reason to believe he was anything but a jerk. But she still loved him.

And he was throwing it away. *For what?*

All this time he had been so sure he knew the answer to that question. There were good reasons why he couldn't give in to the undeniable feelings he had for Gena. But now he wasn't sure they were enough.

Kristen was the biggest reason, of course. She loved him too—she had to in order to put up with the news she had received this summer. The four years they had behind them had been good ones, and he didn't want to throw them away. And he didn't want to break her heart.

Like he was breaking Gena's. Travis tipped his head back against the wall and sighed. He would give anything to not be in this mess—to not have to hurt either one of these women.

He didn't want to hurt Mia, either. She wanted so badly for them to all be together that he couldn't imagine her devastation if things didn't work out. And explaining to her why he was breaking up her family was a conversation he didn't want to have. Fifteen was a tough age, and she had enough to go through without him adding more to it.

In a choice between breaking any woman's heart and his daughter's, there was no contest. It was best to leave the situation alone and hope Gena would forgive him eventually and move on, even if the thought of her finding a new relationship made him ache for his own loss.

It was soon obvious that Gena wasn't going to come out of the bathroom as long as he was there. He had unfinished business with his daughter, so he followed the blare of the radio through the house and up the stairs.

It would be impossible for her to hear his knock over the music, so he opened her door a crack and peeked his head in. "Hey, kiddo. Can I come in?"

Her room was a typical fifteen-year-old's, with clothes draped over a chair and posters of boy bands on the walls. Her pom-poms were tossed in a corner, and her desk was covered in music CDs, most of them made by the boys in the posters.

Mia was lying on her stomach on the bed, idly flipping through a magazine. She gave him a sullen look and a shrug that clearly said *suit yourself.*

Travis went straight to the radio and turned the volume down. Then he pushed some clothes out of the way and sat on the chair. "I didn't want to leave without saying goodbye."

"Leaving to your hotel or leaving for Boston?" She tried to ask the question casually, but he could see the tension in her face and shoulders.

"Back to the hotel," he replied, trying to sound upbeat, which was far from how he was feeling. "I...I overreacted earlier. I was a little harsh. You can do your piano but you can't use your computer or mine for a week."

She shrugged again and he sighed. He'd worked with enough teenagers to know this was their standard form of communication, but it had never been this frustrating when it was somebody else's child.

"I do want you to apologize to Kristen, though."

She nodded, still flipping the pages of the book. He was getting ready to snatch the thing out from under her nose when she looked up. "I don't want you guys to fight."

The breath left his lungs in a rush. *How much did she overhear?* "We just don't see eye to eye on some things. And I don't know much about being a dad, and she knows a lot about being a mom, so it's going to happen. And I don't want you to think it's your fault, because it's not. We just have to learn how to be parents together."

He couldn't decipher the look she gave him. Maybe she just didn't want them arguing over her. But maybe she had overheard a lot more than that and was seeing her dream of having her parents get married so they could all live happily ever after go down the drain.

It only reinforced the fact that having a relationship with Gena would not be healthy for Mia. They were all starting to adjust to their roles in the family and those roles didn't need to change.

He slapped his hands on his thighs and smiled at her. "So are we okay?"

He got the shrug again, but this time a small smile with it. "Yeah, I guess."

"Good." He stood and walked over to the bed to kiss the top of her head. "I'll see you later then."

Gena heard Travis's footsteps come down the stairs and stop in front of the bathroom door. She sat on the closed toilet lid with her face in her hands, trying to stop the steady flow of tears.

It wasn't working. In her mind she kept seeing the horror on his face—over and over again, and it cut through her like a hot blade.

If kissing her made him feel like that, why did he do it again? How could he want her if kissing her had that affect on him?

I wasn't good enough for him then, and I'm not now. She should have thrown him off her property when he and Kristen had first arrived. Mia would still be hers alone and her heart wouldn't be shattering into a billion pieces.

After a few long minutes she heard Travis walk out into the kitchen, then the front door closed behind him. It wasn't until she heard the growl of his pickup's engine and the spray of gravel as he tore out of the driveway that she bent her head to knees and gave in to the wrenching sobs.

Chapter Ten

Gena held the cordless phone in her hand, daring herself yet again to make the call. She had already dialed the number once but hung up before the first ring had ended. Then she had hit the redial four times, each time hitting the OFF button before it could even ring.

"Just call him, already," she said aloud in the empty kitchen.

The worst he could do was say no, and if he had caller ID, she had already embarrassed herself. Before she could change her mind again she turned the phone on and pressed redial. Taking a deep breath, she forced herself to wait through each ring until it was picked up at the other end.

"Hello?"

"Hi, Joe. It's me—Gena."

Joe Kirkwood didn't say anything for a second, then she heard him clear his throat. "Gena, what a surprise! Is everything all right?"

No, everything was not all right. She had spent days feeling sorry for herself, reliving that kiss and the angry words that came after it over and over in her mind.

She was sick of it. She was tired of waiting around for Travis, only to have him sink her further into a pit of despair and confusion. She wasn't going to do it anymore.

"Sure," she said, forcing a cheerful note into her voice. "I called because…well, that new Mel Gibson movie is playing and I really want to see it, but I don't want to go alone. Mia's in Boston with…her dad. I know it's kind of short notice, but I was wondering if you'd like to go with me tonight."

He was silent for so long that she braced herself for a rejection. "I kind of got the impression you and Travis Ryan were…together, if you know what I mean."

Why should he be any less confused about it than I am? she wondered. "We're not a couple, Joe. The only thing we have together is Mia."

"I'll admit I was a little curious about that at the gallery because I've heard he's supposed to marry that Kristen Sinclair from the Boston news channel."

Gena sighed. She had called him to take her mind off Travis Ryan, not to talk about him. "He is. Look—if you're busy tonight, or you don't want to—"

"No!" he interrupted quickly. "A movie sounds great. What time does it start?"

"Twenty after eight. I can meet you outside."

"No, I'll pick you up at eight, and that'll give us plenty of time to buy our tickets."

Gena was pleased to hear the excitement in his voice. Here was a man who actually enjoyed her company and she had her fingers crossed she would feel the same. "That sounds good. See you then."

She hung up the phone and sank into a chair, wondering if she had done the right thing. She wanted to prove to herself Travis Ryan wasn't the only fish in the sea, but was it fair to drag Joe into it?

She had already made up her mind not to hang around the house pining for a man who didn't want her. A date was definitely a step in the right direction. It's not as if she had promised Joe anything. It was just a date—two friends going to a movie together.

And friends were all they would ever be, she realized later in the darkness of the theatre. Joe Kirkwood was a great guy, but she couldn't summon even a spark of desire for him. And she had tried.

He was handsome, but his pale blue eyes didn't seem to reach right into her soul. When he put his hand on her back to guide her to their seats she felt nothing but an urge to move away. And when their hands had brushed over the popcorn bucket she had pulled away before he could entwine his fingers through hers.

Damn you, Travis Ryan, she thought viciously. He didn't want her, but he'd gone and ruined her for any other man.

And Joe knew it, too. He kept glancing at her in the dim light and giving her a sad smile filled with regret. Her heart ached for him but she couldn't feel something that just wasn't there, no matter how much she had hoped to.

When the movie was over they drove back to the Inn in silence. He walked her to the door, and Gena felt a pang of guilt when he leaned close and kissed her cheek.

"I had a good time," she told him, and she meant it for the most part. If only she could have left her thoughts of Travis at home.

"So did I," Joe said. "And I hope you get it all figured out soon."

"So do I," she whispered.

He smiled and rubbed her shoulder. "Until you do, give me a call if you need a friend to see a movie with, okay?"

She watched him drive away and went into the house, cursing Travis with every breath she took.

Travis looked over at Mia with growing concern. She was curled up on his couch, staring off into space. He sensed there was something bothering her, but he couldn't figure out what it was.

She had been fine all day, but was growing more and more quiet as the evening went on. He was beginning to wonder if he had upset her, but he couldn't think of a single thing he'd done wrong.

"Are you nervous about starting school?" he asked when he couldn't stand the silence anymore.

Looking over at him, Mia shook her head. "I love school. I can't wait until Wednesday."

"Then what's eating you?"

She smiled sheepishly and shrugged. "I've never been away from Mom before. I miss her a little."

So do I. He pushed that thought away in a hurry. "Do you want to call her and say goodnight?"

"Yeah." She took the cordless phone from him and punched in the number. "Hi…Donna? Where's Mom?"

Travis waited, listening to Mia's end of the conversation. "Oh… Can you tell her I called? No, nothing's wrong. I just wanted to say hi, and that I miss her. Okay…bye."

"Did your mom go out?" Travis asked in a casual tone he had to struggle for when she had turned off the phone.

"Yeah. She went on a date with Mr. Kirkwood."

The fast-food dinner Mia had insisted on soured in his stomach. She was out on a date with that guy from the gallery.

He should have known there was something between Gena and Joe Kirkwood. The guy's attraction to her had been written all over his face. And it certainly explained why she had overreacted to his touch.

The jealousy was so overwhelming he went into the kitchen. He didn't want Mia to see it on his face and jump to the wrong conclusion—if it *was* the wrong conclusion. He wasn't sure what to think.

He knew he couldn't have it both ways. If she wasn't with him she was free to be with anybody she chose, and he was the one who kept pushing her away. It was his own fault, so he had nobody to blame but himself.

Resting his palms on the counter, he leaned his forehead against the top cabinet. He had no right to be angry or jealous. It didn't even make sense if what he felt for her was only sexual attraction. And it was.

He told himself that so often he almost believed it. That didn't explain why he wanted to put his fist through the birch cabinet in front of him. Why should it matter to him so much if she went out with another man?

After all, it only made his life easier. If there was a boyfriend around the place, he'd be a lot less likely to act on his urges to touch her...to kiss her. Maybe he would even be able to stop thinking about her. Eventually.

"What time is Kristen coming over?" Mia yelled from the living room.

He glanced at the microwave clock. "She'll be here in another half-hour or so."

"Cool. She's going to show me how to do a French manicure."

"That's great, kiddo." He sighed, suddenly not looking forward to an evening spent watching his fiancée bond with his daughter.

Mia started school, and as the days grew shorter and the nights colder, they fell into a comfortable routine that minimized Gena's contact with Travis.

She didn't miss him any less, and she still spent almost every night tossing and turning—dreaming about that kiss in the kitchen. But at least every day wasn't an emotional rollercoaster ride anymore, and she was beginning to think just maybe she would survive this broken heart.

She shivered and set her camera down to button her cardigan. It was getting chilly, even during the day now, and she added getting their winter coats cleaned to the list of things to do.

She picked up the camera again and walked to the far side of the yard, checking the composition through the viewfinder every few feet. Finally she reached a distance where she could get a full shot of the house with the trees surrounding it.

The peak tourist season wouldn't start for another couple of weeks, especially up north, but the leaves were starting to change on the trees around the Inn. She wanted to take the pictures for new brochures before they fell. While the house was attractive even when framed by snow or by flowers, autumn was her favorite.

She took several shots, capturing the large white house surrounded by leaves in shades of gold, orange and crimson. Scattered around the property were some pines, and the glimpses of green in the viewfinder only enhanced the brilliant colors.

Gena heard the truck before she saw it and she turned the camera off. Usually she was in the house when Travis dropped Mia off, but she had gotten the timing wrong this time. Short of ignoring her and driving right by her, he had no choice but to say hello, and she would have no choice but to respond.

His truck turned into the drive and she tried to brace herself emotionally as she walked toward it. Mia got out and waved, her face beaming. Travis also got out, which surprised her. She stopped, took a deep breath, and walked the rest of the distance to the driveway.

"Hi, Mom! Guess what? Dad's taking us apple picking tomorrow!"

She turned to Travis, watching the slight red flush creep over his face. "Us? Is Kristen coming up this weekend?"

"No. I mean you and me and him," Mia said over her shoulder as she walked to the house.

The three of us...apple picking? Remembering her resolve to play it cool—to not wear her heart on her sleeve—she gave him a half-smile. "We're going apple picking?"

Travis looked over his shoulder to make sure Mia was out of earshot. "She told me you guys go every year and I mentioned that I've never gone. She insisted."

"You grew up here. You didn't even go when you were a kid?"

"Nope. It wasn't my mother's idea of fun."

"Oh." Gena wracked her brain trying to come up with some excuse—any excuse— that didn't make it sound like she was avoiding him.

"I think it's important to her," Travis insisted. "It's a family thing—like the movies."

Her face felt hot immediately and she bit down on her lip. The memories of how that first movie night had ended were all too clear in her mind. Then those memories led her mind to that kiss in the kitchen, and she turned away. There was absolutely no way she could let that happen again.

But she couldn't get out of this without looking like a jerk to her daughter, and she didn't want Travis to know he affected her that much—that he could influence her decisions.

"Fine. What time?"

"I told Mia I'd pick you guys up around noon."

That wasn't going to happen. "We'll meet you at the orchard at twelve-thirty. *If* I can get Donna to work. She usually likes a little more notice."

Travis smiled and looked down at his feet. "Actually, Mia already talked to her. She'll be here."

She was out of excuses. "Twelve-thirty, then?"

His eyes were warm, and his voice just a little too low when he said, "I'll see you tomorrow."

She stood where she was long after his truck had pulled out of the driveway. She was going to spend an afternoon with Mia and Travis picking apples. So what? She was a big girl, and she could handle it.

There would be no kissing, she vowed. No kissing, no touching—no tears. She would be…indifferent.

That was a lot easier said than done, she realized when they got out of the car in the orchard's parking lot.

Travis waited near the main barn which served as the store. The day bordered on cold, and he wore a blue fisherman's sweater that accented not only his eyes, but the width of his shoulders and chest.

Gena shivered and she wasn't sure if it was Travis or the weather, but she did wish she had worn something heavier than the cardigan.

"Can we ride the tractor up to the field?" Travis asked, pointing at the trailer piled high with hay bales that was hooked behind an old Massey-Ferguson tractor.

She had to laugh at his boyish enthusiasm. "We usually just walk since Mia got bored with the tractor ride a long time ago, but we can if you want."

"Did you get the bags yet?" Mia asked.

"Bags?" He scowled. "We need bags?"

"How many apples can you stuff down that sweater?" Gena asked in a mocking voice.

"I'll get them," Mia offered, already making her way into the barn.

"Thanks for coming, Gena," he said when they were alone.

"It wasn't my idea."

"I know it wasn't, but I'm still glad you came."

She didn't say anything, so Travis shoved his hands into his pockets and watched the children running around the parking lot.

Shannon Stacey

He had hoped this outing would help them establish a more stable—platonic—relationship, but now he thought that ship might have already sailed. He could tell by the lift of her chin, the rigidity of her spine, that Gena was merely masking the hurt and anger she was no doubt still feeling.

He cleared his throat. "We haven't really had a chance to talk since our…fight in the kitchen."

She whirled to face him, her hazel eyes narrowed. "And we're not going to talk about it now. We're here with our daughter, in case you forgot."

"I didn't forget. I just want to apologize."

"I've heard it before. You can keep your apologies and keep your distance, too."

He was trying to think of something to say when Mia came out with six large paper bags with twine handles. Each was stamped with the name of the orchard and held about ten pounds of apples.

"How many apples do we have to pick?" he asked in mock horror, taking two bags from her.

"Mom uses them for pies and she cans some to use during the winter. We get some sad looking apples at the grocery store."

"How do you know if they have worms?"

Mia laughed and took hold of his arm, dragging him toward the tractor. "Just come on."

Travis helped her up onto the hay bales, his emotions a tangle of happiness and regret. The more time he spent with his daughter, the more he realized how wonderful she was, and how blessed he was to have her in his life.

He also regretted all the lost years. When he saw her saucy grins and stubbornly set chin he imagined what a handful she must have been as a little girl. He would have loved to watch her grow into the amazing young lady she was now.

He turned to help Gena onto the trailer and tamped down those feelings. What was done was done, and he'd promised himself—and Gena—that he would live in the present.

When he extended his hand he saw her hesitate, staring down at his open palm. Then she took a deep breath, put her hand in his and stepped up. He felt a crazy urge to put his hand on her bottom and push, but the thought of getting a verbal dressing-down in public didn't appeal to him.

He satisfied himself with watching her, admiring the generous curve of her behind as she climbed. Then he remembered Mia might be watching him and tore his gaze away. He let go of Gena's hand and hoisted himself up.

The ride up the hill to the orchard was bumpy and they all laughed when Travis almost bounced off the hay bales. He regained his balance and gave them a sheepish grin. "Sorry, I'm new at this."

When they reached the top of the hill Mia ran ahead to a woman sitting at a wooden desk in the middle of the road and came back with three contraptions he had never seen before. They were long sticks with mesh baskets at the top. "What is this for?"

Both women shook their heads at him. "It's to pick the apples from up high, Dad."

"Oh." He took his stick and his bags and followed them until they found a row of trees they liked. Then they set about ignoring him while rapidly filling their bags with luscious red apples.

He followed them up row after row until Gena and Mia had each filled both their bags. His first bag was only half-full, and Gena laughed out loud.

"What have you been doing? You're supposed to be picking apples, not daisies."

He tried to focus on her words instead of her musical laugh, but it wasn't easy. He loved to hear her laugh and it didn't happen often when he was around.

"You can't just take any apple," he said an affronted voice. "You have to check the skin and make sure they don't have any holes, and…"

His words tapered off as his gaze met hers. Her hazel eyes sparkled in amusement and the chilly autumn air added a rosy glow to her cheeks. The light breeze played with her hair, blowing soft auburn wisps across her face.

"You are so beautiful," he whispered before he could stop the words.

Her smile froze in place and the light in her eyes died. She turned away from him and he wanted more than anything to take those words back, but he couldn't. He stepped forward, intending to... *What? What am I going to do?*

Mia cleared her throat, jerking him back to reality. "I'm going to climb the lookout tower. I'll probably be a while."

"We'll be right there," he said.

Gena heard Mia walk away and she sighed, waiting for Travis to say something. *Indifference*, she reminded herself yet again. She couldn't let him see how his words had affected her.

But it was hard. *You are so beautiful.* She couldn't even count the times in her life she wished he would say those words to her. And now he had, but it made no difference. He belonged to another woman, and it would stay that way.

"Why did you go out with Joe Kirkwood a while back?"

Gena spun to face him, hardly believing she had heard him correctly. "How did you know that, and what business is it of yours?"

"I was in the room when Mia called to say goodnight to you and Donna told her where you were. And it *is* my business."

Gena planted her hands on her hips. "How do you figure that?"

He hesitated, a flush climbing his neck, and she wondered if he was still jealous. After all, he had pulled that stupid stunt at the gallery—and now this.

"Well...of course it's my business who you date. You can't have just any guy around Mia. She's my daughter and I don't want strange men near her."

Gena's outburst of laughter was bitter. "Strange men? She has known Joe her entire life. And I didn't marry him—we just saw a movie."

His jaw tightened and he looked down at the ground. "Are you going to see him again?"

"I might," she lied without hesitation. Maybe he wouldn't like taking a back seat to another anymore than she did. "He's very sweet, and he's a *gentleman.*"

Anger flared in his blue eyes. "Did he kiss you?"

"Yes, he did." *On the cheek,* she added to herself. "And I say again—it's none of your business."

He swore and threw his bag of apples on the ground. When he turned to walk away she stepped forward and grabbed his arm. "You don't get it both ways, Travis."

"What are you talking about?" he practically snarled.

"You don't want me but nobody else can have me? It doesn't work that way."

He jerked his arm away. "Fine. Date anybody you want. Sleep with every guy you meet. See if I give a damn."

His words knifed through her and she slapped him hard. Instantly her handprint glowed a soft pink on his cheek. She backed away, her hand raised to cover her mouth in shock. "Travis…"

"I deserved that," he said in a low voice. "But don't you ever do that again."

He started to walk away, then turned back. "We're about done here, I think. I'll get Mia."

She only nodded, unable to get any words past her throat. When he was out of sight in the trees she sat in the grass, covering her face with her hands.

Shame made her face feel hot, and she wondered how she could ever face him again. She had never lost her temper like that before, and she had certainly never struck anybody in anger. But his words had wounded her so deeply she had simply lashed out.

What had she done? Mia would be furious if she found out she had struck her father and it would be hard to miss with her handprint on his face. She prayed it would fade before Mia came down from the tower.

Well, she thought, *I won't have to worry about him wanting to kiss me anymore.*

Chapter Eleven

Mia paced the living room with her hands on her hips and her chin raised. Gena watched her—her own arms crossed—determined not to give in to her daughter's stubbornness.

"I want you and Dad to be there together."

"And I said *no*."

"You guys are my parents. You're supposed to put what I want above your own feelings."

Gena laughed and shook her head. "Where did you read that—some teen magazine advice column? It's not going to happen, Mia. I did the apple picking, but that's it."

She paced in silence for a minute and Gena knew she was regrouping—planning her next attack. But it didn't matter because she was not going to sit beside Travis for two hours in the auditorium.

"You know how much my recitals mean to me," Mia said in a much softer voice. "Just this once I'd like to have you both there. Just once, and I promise I won't ask you again."

"No."

"Mom! You're supposed to be the adult here. How hard can it be to sit with a guy and listen to music for a couple of hours?"

Very hard, Gena thought. *Too hard.*

Mia hadn't said a word about the abrupt end to apple picking, for which Gena was thankful. But she had to have noticed the increased tension between her parents, as well as the fact they had managed to stop speaking to each other altogether.

As hard as that was, she knew it was for the best. She and Travis weren't capable of being friends, and it was about time they both admitted it.

"Why don't you invite your dad to this one and I'll go to the next one?"

Mia stopped pacing. "You have to be there. This will be the first time I play Mozart's *Sonata* in public and you don't want to be there?"

Gena knew this argument was almost over and she was going to lose. "Of course I'm going—"

"And I want Dad there, too."

Her chin still had the stubborn set, but her blue eyes were big and pleading. Gena sighed and surrendered. "Okay, you can invite him."

"Umm...I think you should invite him."

"You can call him in Boston. He's your father."

Mia rolled her eyes. "If I call him he won't believe it's okay with you if he goes. If you call him he'll know. His number is second on the speed dial."

Travis sent up a silent prayer of thanks when the phone rang. He and Kristen had spent the last two hours sitting on the couch in silence, watching some tearjerker of a movie that made no sense to him. "Hello?"

"Hi, it's me…Gena."

Her voice reverberated through his body. He had been thinking about her again, just as he had for days. He wanted to call her, but he hadn't been able to summon the courage. And he didn't know what he would say to her if he did.

"Travis?"

"I'm here," he said quickly, then he glanced at Kristen.

She raised an eyebrow and he shrugged. *It's Gena,* he mouthed and the eyebrow went up another notch. He gave her what he hoped was a reassuring smile and she turned back to the TV.

"Is Mia okay?" he asked Gena, trying to keep his voice very casual.

"Yes, but she's the reason I'm calling. Is this is a bad time?"

"Not at all. Actually you're rescuing me from some sappy movie Kristen's watching." He wanted Gena to know she was there.

Without even looking Kristen reached back and slapped his leg, shushing him. He chuckled and went to the kitchen so he wouldn't disturb her further. And—maybe just a little—so he could be alone with Gena.

She was silent for a long time and he wondered what she was thinking about. Him? Kristen? "Are you still there?"

"Yes. I can call later if you want—since you've got company."

"She's not exactly company, Gena. She spends a lot of time here."

"Right." He heard her take a deep breath, then she continued in a brisk voice. "Mia's piano recital is Saturday night and she wanted me to call and invite you."

"Saturday night? I'm up there anyway and she did mention it already. Of course I'll go."

"She wants us to go...together."

"Oh." He closed his eyes and imagined the three of them, dressed up—he and Gena sitting side by side. He wanted it so bad he could taste it, but it really didn't seem like a good idea. "Is this another of her games?"

"No. I think she's gotten the message as far as that's concerned."

Her voice was cold and he imagined he could hear her adding *and so have I.* And was it his imagination or had Kristen turned down the sound on the television set.

"I can be there," he said, all business.

"I guess... Well, Kristen's invited, of course," Gena said in a tight voice.

Travis nearly groaned aloud. That's just what he needed—Kristen, Gena and Mia together. "I think she has some appointments that afternoon, so she probably can't make it."

"That might be for the best because it's really important to Mia that we go as...her parents," she said. "She worked really hard on the pieces she'll be playing and they're pretty impressive. After Saturday we'll probably take turns or whatever."

"That's fine."

They finalized the details and Travis hung up the phone, trying to ignore the butterflies in his stomach. Even when he went back in to the living room and sat down next to Kristen, he was thinking ahead to seeing Gena again.

More than anything he wished he could go back in time and take back that kiss. Not because he didn't want to kiss her—he *still* wanted to—but because he wanted to erase the hurt he had caused in her eyes. And he wanted to change that moment in the apple orchard.

There were so many things he wanted to explain. He wanted to call her back and tell her that his reaction to the kiss had nothing to do with her. He had been horrified at himself, at his own lack of control. And he had pushed her—purposely— to the breaking point in the orchard. He wanted her to throw him out of her life because he didn't have the strength to do it himself.

His wedding wouldn't take place in October as planned, but he had committed to marrying in Mexico in the spring. Kristen still wore the extravagant diamond he'd sunk into debt to buy her. He was still engaged and he had no business kissing anybody else—especially his ex-wife.

The ex-wife who still loves me. And he was beginning to suspect that, despite all the stern lectures he'd given himself, he was falling in love with her—had probably already fallen.

The thought scared him to the bone. If he admitted to himself he might be falling in love with Gena Taylor, his whole life was going to be turned upside down. Along with the lives of three women who were very important to him—none of whom he wanted to hurt.

But there was no longer any way out of this situation without somebody being left behind. He knew—as much as he didn't want to—that very soon he would have to decide who that was going to be.

"Travis," Kristen said in a low voice.

He jerked himself back into the present and tried to smile at his fiancé. "What, honey?"

"During the time you're here with me, you need to really be *here* with me."

Guilt swept through him and he knew she had to see it, but he lied to her anyway. "Sorry, just thinking about…Mia."

He lifted her hand and kissed the back of it. The diamond winked shards of light back at him.

<hr/>

It was ridiculous to take two vehicles to the recital, so Travis met them at the Inn and they all rode together in Gena's minivan. She wasn't thrilled about sitting next to him in such a confined area, but it couldn't be helped. On top of that, he and Mia had cajoled her into letting him drive.

So she sat in the passenger's seat, her body as rigid as steel. Mia wore the requisite black skirt and white blouse, with low black pumps and a white bow in her hair, but Gena and Travis couldn't look more like a couple if they had signs around their necks.

His blue suit and plum tie were the perfect complements to her navy dress and amethyst jewelry. She thought back to how Mia had urged her towards that outfit and fumed. No doubt she had already seen the suit Travis had brought up to wear and matched them purposely.

Gena didn't believe for a second the scene following Mia's talk with Kristen had taught the girl a lesson. She was just being more subtle in her attempts to play matchmaker for her parents.

It was only a fifteen minute drive to the private school where Mia's piano instructor taught and where they would hold the recital, but it seemed like much more. Mia sat in the far back seat, wearing headphones and humming along to the music, leaving Gena and Travis in awkward silence in the front.

"Relax," he said after a few miles, and Gena gave him a quelling look.

Relax? That was easy for him to say. She hadn't been able to relax since the day he drove Kristen's Mercedes up to her front porch.

"I promise I won't try to kiss you," he said in a low voice.

Heat suffused her face and she stared straight ahead. The thought had crossed her mine once or twice, so she couldn't deny it. But she wasn't about to admit it him, either. Especially with Mia in the car, humming or not.

"Is that supposed to be funny?" she whispered.

She felt his gaze on her for a second before he turned back to the road. "No. You just seem kind of tense, and I thought you might be worried about the possibility."

"There is no possibility. None."

She heard him suck in a breath. "Okay, then."

"For your information, I'm tense because I'm nervous for my...our daughter. She's practiced very hard for tonight and she's devastated when she makes a mistake."

He reached out to pat her hand. "She'll do fine."

Gena froze, her gaze drawn down to the sight of his hand covering hers. The gesture suggested familiarity, even intimacy, and while her flesh drank in the warmth of his touch, her heart shied away from the pain that would follow.

"Don't touch me," she hissed, and he jerked his hand away as if he'd been burned.

She turned her head to stare out her own window, satisfied that her coldness would keep him at bay for a while. At least until she could figure out how to resist him—or if she even could.

There were a lot of students performing, so the auditorium was almost full when they arrived. Mia would be sitting in the second row, behind the beginning students. She gave each of her parents a hug for luck.

"You'll do great, sweetie," Gena whispered near her ear, careful not to mess up her daughter's hair. It had taken them almost an hour to smooth into a twisted ponytail, and then another ten minutes to attach the bow just perfectly.

"Thanks, Mom. I'm really nervous."

Travis enveloped her in his arms, apparently not caring how long it took a teenage girl to prep for an occasion like this. "Don't let them see you sweat."

The instructor was beckoning for Mia to join her class, so she kissed them each again and left. Gena scowled up at Travis. "What kind of encouragement was that?"

He shrugged and gave her a sheepish grin. "I work with athletes, remember?"

They found two seats together toward the back. When they sat, Gena became uncomfortably aware of how Travis's shoulders took up more than their share of space. His arm pressed against her own, forming a little center of shared heat that seemed to radiate through her entire body.

He's marrying another woman, she repeated over and over again in her mind, hoping eventually the thought would stick.

Loving Travis Ryan was as hopeless and painful now as it was fifteen years ago. She was tired of shedding tears and losing sleep over him. Over the last weeks she had tried to tell herself he wasn't worth it, didn't deserve her love. But the more time she spent with him, the more convinced she was that he *was* worth it.

Tensions had been high, of course, but the man had a teenage daughter sprung on him with no warning. He'd turned his personal and professional lives upside down in order to do what he felt was right. He was a good man who'd dealt with the upheaval and confusion the best he could.

And he was simply *the one*. They'd never been lovers in the true sense of the word, but she'd loved him all the same. The whirlwind of pain and confusion that was their brief marriage may have tarnished the memory of her girlish infatuation, but seeing his likeness in Mia every day hadn't let it die completely. But none of what she'd felt for the boy compared to what she felt for the man he'd become.

The program started and Gena focused her attention on the little girl who was so tiny she had to be helped onto the piano bench. She played the most basic of pieces, but she played it well, and the applause at the end was enthusiastic.

As student after student performed, Gena was able to relax and enjoy the music—until about halfway through the intermediate students. The chairs were close together, and she knew Travis was a little cramped. She was still surprised when he shifted in his seat, turning his body more toward her. He lifted his arm and rested it across the back of her seat, the length of it touching her shoulders.

She tensed, ready to give his ears a blistering they wouldn't soon forget, but he whispered, "If you don't let me stretch out a bit, I'll have to get up and walk around. I don't want to be rude."

She bit down on the angry words and simply ignored him. She could hear his breathing now, and she was surprised the beating of her heart didn't drown out the piano melodies. In hopes of calming herself she tried to breathe slowly, but it wasn't easy with his arm practically cradling her.

"Is Mia in the next group?" he asked softly. She nodded stiffly. "Good. With all these people, it's hot as hell in here."

You have no idea, she thought bitterly. When he whispered she could feel the little hot puffs of his breath on her ear, and she shivered, despite feeling downright feverish.

Forcing herself to focus on the stage, she tried to lose herself in the performances, but it was impossible. She was too aware of Travis sitting next to her, the way his body swayed slightly with the music.

How often had she attended these recitals alone—a single mother who sometimes invited a friend? Even with his touch inflaming her senses, she appreciated this moment of togetherness.

This was what she wanted—a real family. Father and mother watching their daughter, silently cheering her on. She wanted Mia to have them both, and she wanted to have Travis in her life. Somebody to share the high moments and the low, to share her joy and her sorrows. Somebody to understand and hold her when Mia left for college.

But it wasn't going to happen, and the ache in her chest was nearly suffocating. *What if I had told him?* If she hadn't let him leave that day without telling him she *was* pregnant, would they be sitting here now as man and wife, maybe with Mia's brothers or sisters sitting next to them?

Tears blurred her vision, and she forced herself to remember it didn't matter now. It was too late, and she could never bring that moment back. Now all she could do was keep repeating her mantra— *He's marrying Kristen Sinclair.*

Finally it was Mia's turn and Travis lifted his arm from her shoulders. Even in her anxiety for her daughter she missed its warmth, and she silently cursed herself for a fool. Then the room filled with the Beethoven's *Moonlight Sonata*, and she forgot everything else but her daughter's music.

She sat upright in her seat, her hands clenched into fists. *Please...please let her get through this okay*, she prayed silently. She tapped her foot, silently keeping the beat as Mia moved through the movements.

As the piece—played flawlessly—came to a close Travis slipped his hand over Gena's and squeezed. She turned to him and her face beamed with so much joy and pride his heart ached in his chest.

"She did it," Gena whispered, and then smiled.

That smile. The one that had haunted him for fifteen years.

But this one wasn't for him. It was for their daughter. When Mia was finished playing the Mozart piece, she would pull away from him again, and he couldn't blame her after the way he had treated her.

He had no right to expect Gena to love him now. He had pushed her away—battered her emotions—because he wanted her. It was selfishness, and it didn't matter that trying to keep her at a distance was the right thing to do.

That didn't make it hurt any less, for either of them. He had spent more time than he cared to confess missing the sound of her voice. He wanted her to smile at him and laugh with him. He wanted to scoop her up in his arms and kiss the daylights out of her without his conscience screaming.

Halfway through Mozart's *Sonata*, Travis admitted to himself he was hopelessly in love with Gena Taylor. He tried to pass it off as the result of an evening of emotionally-charged music, but it didn't work.

I love Gena. He was surprised to feel a rush of relief when he finally said the words silently to himself. *I'm in love with her.*

And I've already lost her. She couldn't even stand his touch in the car on the way over and her voice had been downright venomous.

If only he had recognized his feelings earlier—before he took her love and threw it back in her face—he'd have a better chance at convincing her it was safe for her to continue loving him. But convince her he would—very soon.

First he had a trip to Boston to make. As soon as they got back to the Riverside Inn he would get in his truck and drive to Kristen's. He didn't want to hurt her. His love for Kristen had been real, and he already regretted the pain this would cause her. But she wasn't stupid, and somehow he thought she knew it was coming.

He couldn't marry her now. Because he did care for her, he had too much respect for her to say vows he didn't mean. And once that was over, and he had figured out what to do with his practice, he could come back and begin the slow process of earning Gena's love.

He held her hand through Mozart's *Sonata*, then reluctantly let her go so they could join in the applause for their daughter. *And I will earn it,* he promised himself as he looked down at her flushed, joyful face.

※

Gena sighed and crossed her arms. "You guys have been arguing about this for ten minutes. Pick something, already."

Travis and Mia both turned to give her almost identical shushing looks. She rolled her eyes and they both grinned.

"This is serious stuff," Travis explained. "We all agree on the pepperoni and the bacon, but you want mushrooms and Mia wants onions and I want grilled chicken."

"Grilled chicken? That's an entree, not a pizza topping."

"Have you ever tried it?"

Mia waved her hand between them. "Hello? If you guys start we'll never get to eat. I'll try the chicken. So—" she turned to the guy behind the counter "—one large pizza with pepperoni and bacon, half with mushrooms and half with grilled chicken."

"You shouldn't get mushrooms on a pizza," Mia grumbled when they had found a table. "They slide around and they'll end up on our side of the pizza."

"They're good for you," Gena insisted. "They're vegetables."

"They're fungus," Travis and Mia said at the same time.

"You owe me a Coke," Mia said, punching him in the arm. "And I have to go to the little girl's room. Be right back."

Gena gave her a stern look and Mia returned it with one of wide-eyed innocence. "What? I really do have to pee. I haven't gone since before the recital."

Left alone at the table, Gena noticed Travis seemed more relaxed than he had in a long time, and she couldn't help but wonder why. He looked like a man who had gotten a big load off his mind.

Maybe it was the relief of Mia's performance being behind them. It was his first recital, after all, and the nerves that came with watching a child perform in public might have been overwhelming for him.

But when he looked at her she saw the warm glow in his blue eyes and butterflies skittered through her stomach. He looked like a man with a surprise up his sleeve. A good one.

Travis leaned forward, resting his elbows on the table. "I think you and I should start over."

That's it? Gena smirked and shook her head. "We already tried that. It didn't work."

"I want us to be friends."

Pain squeezed her heart, but she was thankful her eyes remained dry. She was determined never to cry in front of this man again—especially if he was the cause of her tears.

I don't want to be your friend, she thought. *I want more.* She wanted what his kisses had promised, but failed to deliver.

"This is as good as it's going to get, Travis. I'm not letting you get close to me again."

Gena tried to believe her own words, but she couldn't. She only hoped they sounded convincing to him. For her own heart's sake he had to believe she didn't want him—wouldn't let him kiss her again if he tried.

"If for Mia, if nothing else," he insisted.

"Mia needs what we have now. We went to her recital together, we're being polite, and she's having a good time." He touched her hand and the zap of electricity that jolted her heart made Gena jerk away. "Stop it, Travis. I mean it. I don't want you any closer than arm's reach."

For a quick moment she actually thought he looked hurt, but then Mia reappeared and the moment passed. The pizza came and they laughed and ate and talked, every second of it adding to the lead weight in Gena's stomach.

This was how it should always be. She imagined how they must look to the strangers surrounding them. A happy family, dressed up for some occasion, laughing over pizza. None of them knew how her heart was breaking or that she cried inside almost every moment of the day.

Back in the van, Travis wondered how he was going to convince Gena that he loved her if she wouldn't even entertain the notion of being friends.

He understood why, of course. In his determination to keep Kristen and Mia from being hurt, he'd had very little consideration for Gena's feelings. He knew he had hurt her—repeatedly.

Way to go, Trav. You've probably lost her for good this time. But he wasn't going to give up without a fight. He reached over and slapped her thigh. "Quit sulking."

She glared at him in the flickering light of the streetlamps. "I am *not* sulking."

"Yes, you are. You're pouting because I'm driving your car."

Gena laughed, sparking a flicker of hope in his chest. "That's ridiculous."

"Good, because I'm a good driver." He jerked the wheel to the right and Mia squealed in the back seat. "See?"

"Don't do that to my van," Gena scolded, but he could hear the amusement in her voice.

Travis tapped the brake several times, making the van lurch down the road. "Really, I *am* a good driver."

"Stop...it," Gena managed to say. She and Mia were giggling in earnest now.

Travis basked in the warmth of their laughter, wishing he the drive could longer. He stopped at each of the three driveways before the Inn. "Oops, that's not it. Nope, this isn't the one..."

Gena was doubled over in her seat, holding her stomach, when Travis finally pulled into her driveway. He wasn't surprised when the laughter died. He saw the silver Mercedes with Massachusetts plates and his spirits plummeted. Kristen was back.

Chapter Twelve

Travis turned off the engine and they all sat for a second, the tension instantly palpable. Gena felt the joy rush out of her night as surely as if it had been sucked into a vacuum.

The fairy tale evening was over. The mantra may not have been enough to keep her from dreaming of the family they could be, but having Kristen Sinclair actually present accomplished that with no trouble.

Travis was very quiet, sitting as still as she was. She wondered why he wasn't more excited to see the woman he loved and was going to marry. Stealing a sideways glance at him, she saw he didn't even look happy about it.

"Well, we can't sit in the van all night." She picked her purse up off the floor and opened her door. "You've got company, so we'll get inside."

They all got out of the van just as Kristen stepped out of the shadows of the porch. She didn't look happy, but Gena couldn't say as she blamed her. She probably didn't look very happy herself.

"Hi," Kristen said, walking down the steps. "I rearranged my appointments so I could come, but you'd already left, Travis. So I thought I'd drive up anyway, but I missed you guys and the woman watching the Inn didn't know where it was. Your cell was off, of course."

"My instructor taped it," Mia said. "I was almost perfect, and when I get the tape we can watch it together."

Gena's heart twisted at the open invitation in her daughter's voice. Sharing her daughter with Travis was one thing, but sharing her with another mother was hard to swallow. Maybe especially hard considering she was also in love with the woman's fiancé. She wasn't sure which was worse—sharing a daughter or sharing a man.

"We should go inside," Gena said, putting her arm around Mia. "These heels are killing me."

Gena shepherded her daughter to the door, but she couldn't resist looking back. She wished she hadn't. Travis placed a light kiss on Kristen's lips and her stomach tightened into a knot. She could have happily gone to her grave without ever seeing that.

Of course he kissed her, she scolded herself. *He loves her and he's going to marry her.*

"You guys looked like you were having a good time," Kristen said with a slight edge to her voice.

"Yeah," Travis replied, looking past her to Gena. "We stopped for pizza, and...it was fun."

Kristen turned and followed his gaze and Gena saw her eyes narrow. She decided it was time to leave them alone. She opened the screen door Mia had allowed to swing shut behind her.

"You need to come home, Travis," she heard Kristen say bluntly. *Home.* "No more games. I want you to come home with me and Mia can come and visit anytime she wants."

Gena stepped into the house, but paused when she heard Travis's reply. "I was actually going back to Boston as soon as I left here. I wanted to see you."

His words slammed Gena, knocking the breath out of her. She didn't know why—she knew he loved Kristen. He was going to marry her. But hearing the gentleness in his voice, knowing he had been thinking about Boston the whole time they had laughed—when he was gazing at her with so much warmth and humor—was too much for her.

She swung the front door closed behind her with enough force to rattle the pictures on the wall. Then she leaned back against it, trying to fight the sudden need to cry. She failed, and that only made her even more angry.

Damn him, she thought as the tears flowed over her cheeks. She was sick of this ride and she wanted off. First desire, then pain, then anger. More pain, then the laughter, and now the worst pain. Enough was enough.

She checked with Donna to make sure the guests hadn't had any problems during her absence, then went into the kitchen where she found Mia getting a drink.

She looked up from the soda she was pouring and scowled, looking so much like her father Gena had to look away. "Mom? Are you okay?"

"Sure, sweetie. I just...I'm tired, I guess."

Mia set her glass down with a thud. "I'm not stupid, Mom, and I'm not blind."

Gena felt her moist cheeks grow hot. This was not a conversation she wanted to have with her—their—daughter. "Mia, I'm fine. Really, I am."

"I'm sorry if my...scheming hurt you. It was dumb, and I didn't even realize that maybe you had feelings for Dad."

One hiccupped sob escaped her. "Sweetheart, it has nothing to do with you. I'm just..."

Her words tapered off, and she grabbed a paper towel to wipe her eyes. She looked at her daughter, realizing her little girl was almost a woman now, and probably already knew a little about broken hearts.

The tears began flowing again, faster than she could mop them up with the paper towel. "Yes, I'm in love with your dad, Mia. I think I always have been, and some part of me always will be, but I promise you it has nothing to do with *your* relationship with him."

Mia lip trembled and her eyes welled up with tears. Gena stepped closer and pulled her into her arms, rocking gently from side to side.

"This really sucks," Mia said into her shoulder.

Gena laughed through her tears. "I agree."

"Why don't you go up to bed? I'll say goodnight to Dad and lock up. Donna's going to stay over since there's an empty room."

"I think I will." She gave Mia a kiss, hugged her again, and opened the door to their rooms.

"Mom?" Gena stopped and looked over her shoulder. "I'm sorry all this happened."

"Me too, sweetie." She turned and walked to the stairs, hoping it wouldn't take long to cry herself to sleep.

Outside, the night air was growing chilly and Travis shoved his hands in his pocket. He tried to look Kristen in the face, but it wasn't easy. "Why don't we go back to the hotel? There's no sense in standing out here in the driveway."

She shook her head, and he saw the determination in her eyes. "I think I'll go back to Boston tonight."

"Kristen, you just drove all the way here. You can't turn around and go back now. I'll get you your own room and we'll talk."

He didn't want to talk—was dreading it—but he knew the time had come. If any of them were to have a chance at happiness, he had to be honest with everybody—even if it hurt.

But he didn't want to tell her he was in love with his ex-wife while they were standing in the woman's driveway. It wasn't the time, and it definitely wasn't the right place. But he couldn't go on this way anymore. He'd made his decision, and now all he wanted to do was go after Gena.

The slamming of the door had echoed in the deepest chambers of his heart. There was a finality to it, as if she had just closed him out of her life forever. But he couldn't go to her until he had resolved his relationship with Kristen, and he couldn't do that here.

Kristen looked tired and upset, and guilt tugged hard at his conscience. He still cared about her, and the image of her driving back to Boston after hearing what he had to tell her was disturbing. He couldn't do that to her.

"I'll follow you home. We'll talk there."

She hesitated, and he got the impression she didn't want to have this conversation any more than he did. Her expression confirmed his suspicion that she already knew their relationship was coming to an end.

"All right, Travis. But spend the time thinking about what it is you want, because when we get home we're going to make some decisions."

I want Gena. The words were on the tip of his tongue, but he bit them back and nodded. Fishing his truck keys out of his pocket, he cast a glance up at the window on the second floor. It was Gena's, and though it was dark, he was sure she was in her room, probably cursing him to the heavens.

"I have to say goodbye to Mia and then I'll be ready."

Kristen got in her car, but she didn't start it, so he assumed she would wait for him. He walked into the house and smiled a greeting to

Donna, who was still behind the desk filing some paperwork. He found Mia at the kitchen table, her eyes red from recently shed tears.

"Hey, kiddo."

"Kristen looks pretty mad."

He nodded. "She's a little upset, but we're going back to Boston tonight, so we'll get everything straightened out."

He wanted to tell her. She would be thrilled to find out her father was going home to end his engagement so he would be free to confess his love to her mother. But he held back. This was between him and Gena, and he didn't want to drag Mia—and her hopes—into it.

The possibility that Gena would throw his love back in his face was very real. The thought scared him, but he knew he had only himself to blame. A woman could only take so much, and she had taken more than her share of heartbreak from him.

"I'll call you tomorrow."

She only nodded, so he leaned down and kissed the top of her head. "I'll be back here as soon as I can, okay? I'm not sure when it will be, but I will call you."

"Okay. I love you, Dad."

"And I love you, kiddo. So much it blows my mind sometimes." He stood behind her and wrapped his arms around her, resting his chin on her head. "Is your mom around?"

Mia stiffened, and Travis sighed. She knew he was hurting Gena and it wounded him to imagine what she must think of that.

"She went to bed. I don't think she wants company right now."

Again he thought about telling her. She would understand then, and he wouldn't feel like such a heel. But it was for the best this way. No sense in getting the girl's hopes up if he had lost Gena for good.

"Tell her I said goodbye, okay? And I'll see you soon."

When he stepped back into the yard Kristen started her car and put it in gear without even looking at him. Travis opened the door of his truck, then cast one last glance up at the window. His breath caught when he saw her looking down at him.

Her face was blank, expressionless, and it shook him to the bone. He held her gaze for a minute, then she stepped back and let the curtain fall.

She was gone. And he didn't know if he could get her back.

Travis had to stop for gas, so Kristen was already settled in when he let himself into her apartment. She sat on the couch with her feet tucked under her and only one dim lamp lit. The diamond ring sat on the center of the glass table.

She knows it's over. He wasn't sure if he felt more relief or guilt, but it didn't matter. The fact that Kristen knew what he was going to tell her didn't make it any easier.

He tossed his keys on the phone stand and walked over to the couch, sitting down next to her. Leaning forward, he picked up the ring and rolled it between his fingers.

"When you pulled into the driveway you were all laughing," Kristen said in an unusually soft voice. "I saw her face when she saw my car. And I saw your face, too."

"I'm sorry, Kristen." His eyes felt damp, and he had a hard time getting the words through his throat. "I swear I never meant for this to happen."

"Are you in love with her?"

"Yes—" he turned to face her "—but I...I've just figured that out. I don't think I've lied to you."

She gave him a sad smile. "I thought about this on the way home and I realized something. When I found out who she was, I was angry. When you told me you had kissed her, I was angry. I've been very angry."

"I know. I'm so—"

She held up her hand to silence him. "Even all the tears I've cried were because of anger."

"You have every right to be angry. I've been a jerk—to both of you—and you didn't deserve this."

"But it wasn't *hurt*, Travis. You have been falling in love with that woman and all I've felt is jealous anger."

He didn't understand what she was trying to tell him. Of course she would feel jealous anger. The same emotions he had felt when he saw the way Joe Kirkwood looked at Gena that night at the gallery.

"Don't you see, Travis? I want to love a man so much that even the *thought* of him kissing another woman tears my heart out. I want to watch him looking at some other woman the way you looked at Gena and feel like a knife has been stuck in my chest.

"If the man I love has to go away for a weekend, I want to wonder how I can survive it. You've been gone all this time and…I've just been plain old mad. I want to love a man so much I would rather die than have him leave me."

She rested her hand on his knee. "You're not that guy, Travis." Her voice broke as her eyes filled with tears. "I wish you were, but you're not."

He looped his arm around her shoulders and pulled her close to him, resting his chin on her head. Several of his tears fell to rest on her hair. "I'm going to miss you, Kristen. I've loved you for a long time. And I *have* loved you."

"I've loved you, too," she said against his chest, "but we don't have what it takes. You and Gena do, and when I'm done being mad as hell I'll probably wish you all the best."

His chest heaved as he sighed deeply. "Why does a little part of me wish we'd never gone to New Hampshire?"

She lifted her face to his. "Because it would have been easier. We'd be getting married soon, and we would have some kids. We would have lived to be old, boring, married people together."

He kissed her forehead and smiled. "We would have had a good life together."

"Yes, but somewhere down the road, even without Gena, some part of both of us would have realized we settled. We're not soul mates."

He held her close again. "So, now what?"

She shifted in his arms and sighed. "Now you go get your toothbrush out of my bathroom."

Gena sat in the miniature wooden chair and groaned. "When are you going to get some real furniture in here? I feel like a Munchkin."

Jill laughed and set down the pile of books she was supposed to be putting away. "This is the children's room, silly. If you want a comfy chair go sit in the reference section."

"Maybe I can find one of those how-to books for getting my life out of the toilet."

"Not good, huh?

Gena tried to smile, but she couldn't quite manage it. "He's gone—he left last night. For good this time, I think."

Jill pulled up another little chair and sat down. "What do you mean? He's going to see Mia, isn't he?"

"Yeah. She'll go visit, and he'll come up here for school events and recitals and stuff. I mean he left...me."

Jill leaned over and gave her a quick hug. "I'm sorry, hon. But you knew it was going to happen sooner or later."

"I guess I was hoping for later."

"Tell me what happened."

Gena took a deep breath and told her the entire story. She felt stupid telling it—Jill had warned her, after all—but she managed to get it out. The only thing she left out was the sweatshirt.

She had found it in the laundry days ago—a worn sweatshirt with Boston College emblazoned on the front. When she asked Mia about she said she had been cold one night and Travis lent it to her. She had forgotten to give it back.

Last night, after what felt like hours of crying, she had retrieved it from the folded pile and slipped it over her flannel pajamas. The detergent hadn't been able to completely wash away his scent, and wrapped in its warmth and comfort she had finally been able to sleep. She wasn't about to tell Jill about that. She felt foolish enough about it without her best friend laughing at her.

"I don't think a book's going to help," Jill said when she was finished, giving her a sad smile.

"I should have listened to you that day in the park. I could have tossed him out and put Mia on a bus to Boston whenever she wanted to see him."

Jill reached over and patted her hand. "It wouldn't have helped. You were already in too deep by then. You would still be crying yourself to sleep every night."

"Yeah. I've done a lot of that lately."

His lips devoured hers, and she gloried in the realization that this man wanted her—loved her—and she was going to spend forever with him.

"I love you," she whispered against his mouth.

"Good, because—"

Whatever he had been about to say was lost in the screech from the top of the stairs. Mia flew down the staircase, her nightgown billowing around her ankles. She threw herself on top of them, kissing them both and leaving her own tears behind.

"I knew it! I knew you guys loved each other." She wrapped her arms around them and Gena felt a rush of joy, despite the fact she was quickly running out of air.

"Okay, get up," she gasped. "I can't breathe."

"How about me?" Travis said, then laughed. "I'm on the bottom."

Mia got up and hauled them to their feet. "I'm so happy. I love you guys so much."

Gena embraced her daughter, their tears mingling. "And we love you so much, too."

They heard footsteps in the kitchen and Gena shushed them before she went to the door. "Mr. Carson? Did we wake you?"

The still half-asleep man rubbed his face. "Is everything all right down here? It sounds like somebody's being murdered."

"No, I'm not being murdered. I'm getting married!"

"Oh." He turned and started walking back the way he had come. "Well, all right, then."

"Maybe now that he's gone it won't be so bad," Jill said, trying to sound hopeful. "Or maybe he'll call off his engagement and come back."

Gena didn't want to hear that. She spent a lot of time convincing herself that wasn't a possibility and she didn't need the false hope. "I doubt it."

"It happens. I should know, remember?"

"But you didn't love him. That's why you left him. Travis loves Kristen."

"Okay." Jill stood and picked up the stack of books to sort them alphabetically. "Why didn't you tell me you went out with Joe Kirkwood?"

Gena's cheeks felt hot and she ignored Jill's chuckle. "It was no big deal. We went to a movie."

"And who asked who?"

"I invited him. I was trying to—" she paused, shaking her head "—I was trying to make myself fall in love with someone other than Travis Ryan, I guess."

Jill laughed. "That's pathetic. It didn't work, did it?"

"You know it didn't." Gena reached over and messed up the neat stack of books. "And I'm not pathetic."

"So, tell me about it."

She shrugged. "There's not much to tell. We went to the movies and I spent the whole night thinking about Travis. Joe was pretty nice about it, though."

"He's a sweet guy."

"So why couldn't I fall in love with him? Why does it have to be a selfish, arrogant, uncaring jerk who is in love with a beautiful, big shot news anchor?"

"Just lucky, I guess. How's Mia taking this whole thing? Does she know how you feel about him?"

Gena sighed. "She knows. And in her words—she thinks it sucks."

Jill laughed again. "Sorry. I know it's not funny. Poor kid."

"I guess it'll be better for her now. There can't really be tension between her parents if her parents don't see each other, right?"

"Right. Hey, did I tell you the old bat's leaving?"

Gena almost fell out of her chair. "Mrs. Bright is retiring?"

"Retiring?" Jill repeated with a snort. "She's eighty-three years old. I think retirement has come and gone. But I don't care. She's leaving, and I'm going to be head librarian soon."

"Really? Did she tell you that?"

Jill shrugged. "The trustees want to search for somebody, but who wants to move to this dinky town? I've worked here for years and I've been doing her work for most of it."

"Congratulations, hon." Gena tried to pay attention as Jill went on and on about the promotion that was almost hers, but her mind strayed back to Travis—as it almost always did now.

Somehow she didn't think distance was going to be enough. So far, knowing he was three hours away in the arms of his fiancée had done nothing to ease the constant ache in her chest. She had tried to see things logically, with some amount of reason, but nothing helped.

All she could do was hope time would slowly allow the pain to fade into a sad memory, just as it had done fifteen years ago.

⬛

Travis managed almost twenty-four hours before he reached for the phone.

He wanted to hear her voice—craved the sound of it. It would be easy enough to call since Mia had programmed her number on the speed dial. Two buttons and he could talk to her.

But what would he say to her? He didn't want to give her the news of his broken engagement over the phone. Gena would only accept all or nothing—if anything—and he wasn't quite ready to offer everything yet. He still had a few loose ends to tie up.

Just a phone call, he thought. He could say hi and make some small talk before asking to speak to Mia. Even a few minutes would give him a chance to hear her voice and judge how angry she was. Maybe there would be a hint of longing and he would know he hadn't lost her completely.

Before he could change his mind he turned the phone on and punched the buttons. It rang three times before he heard Gena's terse greeting on the other end.

"Gena? It's Travis."

He heard her quick intake of breath, then she was silent for what seemed like a long time, but was probably only seconds. "Mia already went to bed."

Short, abrupt—to the point. His heart sank at the total lack of warmth in her voice. "How is she?"

"She's fine. She misses you and she'll be sorry to hear you called so late."

"How are you?"

She was quiet again, then she said in a too polite voice, "I'm fine, thank you."

He could feel the cold shoulder even over the telephone line and it scared him. Had the scene with Kristen really been the last straw? He wouldn't—couldn't—believe that. "I—I just wanted…I called to see how everything was going, and…"

"Everything's fine. It's late, Travis, so I'll tell Mia you called and she'll call you back when she can."

"Wait—" he wasn't ready to let her go yet "—I miss you, Gena."

Her hesitation this time was so long he wondered if she was just going to pretend he hadn't said it. Then he heard the soft click of the line being disconnected and understood. She was gone.

Travis turned off the phone and sank back against the couch. He had lost her. With a vicious curse he flung the phone against the wall, then covered his face with his hands.

Chapter Thirteen

Gena screamed when a body flew past her and landed in the giant pile of leaves she had gathered on the front lawn. With her heart hammering in her chest she reached her foot out and kicked the body in the butt.

"Mia Dawn Taylor! I spent all afternoon raking those leaves."

A giggle emerged from the pile, then her daughter sat up, bright autumn leaves clinging to her hair and blue Nordic sweater. "And I worked hard at school all day. Come on—"

Before Gena could react, Mia grabbed her arm and pulled her down into the pile next to her. She struggled, weak from laughter, and finally managed to sit up, looking as colorful as her daughter.

They laughed together while Gena picked leaves out of their hair. "How was school today?"

"Good."

"That's it? Just good?" Gena heard the underlying tension in her voice and frowned. "Come on—what's bothering you?"

"Dad called last night."

"Is everything okay?"

"Yeah…I guess."

They both flopped back and stared at the sky, just as they had done when Mia was a little girl. Gena was silent, knowing Mia would tell her mother what was wrong in her own good time.

And Mia would also pass on any information she needed to know. Like the fact that he was very busy, and that's why he hadn't been up for three weeks. Like the fact that he had initiated the paperwork to change Mia's name to Mia Dawn Taylor-Ryan, an action she wasn't entirely on board with yet, but her daughter wanted. She tried to tell herself it was good—communicating through Mia was hard on the family, but healthy for herself.

She did miss him, though. So much that the heavy ache in her heart was constant now, but she knew she could live with it. She *had* lived with it.

She didn't need anybody to tell her the obvious. Kristen had convinced him it was time to go home and play the dutiful husband-to-be, and he had gone. A little over three weeks ago, and she had felt every day of it like a century in her heart.

She didn't want him back in her life—didn't think she could survive it—but not having him was almost as hard. She hadn't even heard his voice since the night he called and she hung up on him. The morning after she had installed a separate phone line in Mia's room. If she was home she could talk to him, if not he could leave her a message. Gena never had to speak to him.

If only she could get him out of her mind as easily. Over and over again she replayed the night of the recital. His arm draped casually around her shoulders, the feel of her hand in his…the way he and Mia had looked at her at the pizza counter and their laughter in the van.

She missed him, and she hated herself for it. But there was no magic product made that could scrub him out of her memory, so she just tried to soldier on, dealing with Mia and her cheerleading and piano practices. There was the onslaught of leaf-peepers—the tourists who flocked north to see the White Mountains in full fall splendor—to tend to.

"You're still in love with him, aren't you?" Mia asked softly.

Gena lifted a handful of leaves and let them fly away in the light breeze. "It doesn't go away that easily."

Mia rolled and propped her head on her hand so she could look down at her mother. "I'm sorry if I pushed it."

"I told you before it wasn't you. It just happened. So what did he say on the phone?"

Mia flopped back into the leaves. "He's got some kind of legal stuff to do, so he doesn't know when he'll be able to come. He said he will as soon as he can."

"Legal stuff?" The custody kind of legal stuff? Suddenly it was hard to breathe. "Did he say what kind?"

"Something to do with his practice, I think. I really miss him a lot."

No matter how much she cursed him as a man, Gena knew Travis wasn't the kind of father who would abandon his daughter. "He'll be here soon, sweetie. Your father loves you very much, and he won't let how I feel about him keep him away from you, if that's what you're thinking."

"I know." Mia sighed and sat up. "It just would have been so nice if he had fallen in love with you, too."

Gena turned her face away and bit hard on her lip. It was too painful—too fresh—to talk about, and she didn't want to discuss her broken heart with anybody, even her daughter.

Above all, she didn't want to speak badly of Mia's father. He was a good dad, and Mia loved him. That was a separate issue, and she didn't want her feelings about Travis to influence their daughter.

"Well, he didn't," she said finally. "And that's that. So what are your plans for the evening? After homework and piano, of course."

"If you want I'll babysit the guests tonight. Why don't you call Jill and see if she wants to go out."

Gena laughed and slapped Mia's leg. "Don't let them hear you say that. And you're not staying alone in the house with the guests until you're older. Like thirty. Now let's bag up these leaves you made a mess out of."

Maybe she should ask Donna to cover for her. It would do her good to get out of the house. Jill was always good for a laugh, and she desperately needed one. Maybe she'd even meet somebody else.

There is nobody else. Her heart had long ago decided it belonged to Travis Ryan, for better or for worse. It was too bad it had turned out to be for the worse.

Travis turned off the highway exit and patted his pocket for the hundredth time since he left Boston. It was still there.

He felt as nervous as he had on that first drive up after meeting Mia—wondering what he should say and hoping he would be enough. Only this time it wasn't his daughter he was concerned about.

Although it was only ten o'clock, the town was almost deserted, and it felt eerie to a guy who had lived in Boston for so many years. He'd already begun falling back into the small town rhythm during his visits each week, but now he'd have to fully embrace is as this would be his home.

If she'll have me. He tried to push that thought away. She had to, or he had no idea how he was going to live the rest of his life.

He pulled into McDonald's and ordered a burger and a coffee, which he sat at a picnic table to eat. The night was growing colder, but he needed the fresh air to calm his nerves.

It had taken almost a month to finalize all the arrangements that needed to be made. He sold his apartment and most of his furnishings. He found a therapist to take over his practice and walked him through the initial two weeks. Then there were contacts in New Hampshire to be made and reams of legal documents to fill out. Real estate forms, loan forms, legal documents to transfer his practice, application forms, rental forms. He didn't think he'd ever signed his name so many times in a year, never mind a month.

The only one he hadn't complained about was the document that would lead to his daughter having his name. He had asked Mia, but hadn't asked Gena because Mia said she still wouldn't speak to him. But she had signed the documents with no fuss and it would be finalized soon.

He realized he had missed Mia more than he ever thought it possible to miss another person. He missed Gena, too—so much his heart ached with it—but without Mia he felt as if a part of himself was gone.

They didn't know he was coming. He couldn't say anything to Gena. When he offered himself to her it had to be freely, with nothing tying him down—calling him back to Boston. He thought that was the only way she might believe he truly meant what he was going to say to her.

And he hadn't told Mia for two reasons. Mostly he didn't want her to tell Gena, giving her the opportunity to turn him down before he even got the chance to try. And he didn't want to get Mia's hopes up, only to have them dashed.

He loved them both—needed them both—and now he was ready to give them what they needed from him.

So, get off your butt and go see them. He threw the empty hamburger wrapper away and got in his truck. After taking a few more sips of the coffee, he started the ignition.

In a few minutes he would know whether the last month of work had been in vain. He patted his pocket again for good luck and put the truck in gear.

Gena heard the truck as it came up the hill and dropped the book in her lap. It sounded like Travis's truck and she cursed herself for a fool. How many times in the last month had she thought she heard his truck? She even heard it in her sleep.

But this time it pulled into the driveway. She threw off the covers and ran to her window, her pulse quickening. Pulling back the curtain, she looked down and saw Travis's truck.

Don't be an idiot, she told herself. He was there to see Mia, and that was the only reason. If she stayed in her room he probably wouldn't even ask about her.

He was getting out and she drank in the sight of him like a woman dying of thirst. She pressed her fingertips to the glass, her lips silently forming his name. Inhaling deeply, she felt a sharp pang of loss for the love she couldn't have.

Then she noticed he had a bundle of roses in his hand. And the back of his truck was mounded high and covered with a tarp, and it was hooked to a small U-Haul trailer. *What is he doing?*

He looked up, and she felt his blue gaze touch hers. She rested her forehead on the window pane and closed her eyes for a second, wondering if maybe she was seeing things—having a dream she didn't want to wake up from.

She opened them and he was still there, looking up at her window as though she was Rapunzel in her tower. His mouth was moving, but she couldn't hear him.

With trembling fingers she fumbled at the window latch, then slid it up with a bang. It took her another second to open the screen, then she stuck her head through the window.

"Travis, what are you doing?"

"You want me to say it again?"

"The window was closed, so I couldn't hear you. And stop yelling or you'll wake the guests."

"I love you, Gena Taylor," he bellowed at the top of his lungs.

Gena jerked her head up, sure she couldn't have heard him correctly, even if he *was* yelling. She smashed the back of her head on the bottom of the sash and yelped in pain.

"Travis, what...I'm coming downstairs. And be quiet!"

She was halfway down the stairs before the full impact of what he had said hit her, and she almost stumbled. He had just shouted his love for her to the whole world. Granted, everybody was asleep, but it counted.

She sank down onto a step and rested her head on her knees, biting her lip to keep from crying. She had no idea what to say—what to do—but she knew there was no way her heart could survive another direct hit. And she'd never suspected, even for a second, he was in love with her.

She wasn't sure when she began to sob, or how long she sat there before Travis entered the house and he found her, still crying on the steps. He knelt on a step below her, trying to peer up into her face.

"Gena? What's wrong? I thought you were coming outside. Hey, that's my sweatshirt."

She lifted her head and swiped at her eyes. "What are you doing to me now, Travis?"

"I love you, Gena. I *love* you."

More tears spilled over and she shook her head. "Then why did you go? Why did you leave and not come back for a month?"

"I had to…I owed Kristen an explanation, and I didn't want to do it here. That's over. Mutually, actually."

Gena pulled the sleeves of his sweatshirt down over her hands and scrubbed her eyes and cheeks. "What's all that in your truck?"

He shifted to sit on the step and rested his hand on her leg. Gena felt its warmth and didn't pull away. *Maybe…*

"It's everything I own in the world." He laughed nervously. "I'm home, if you'll have me."

She pushed her hair back, shaking her head. "Home? You can't live here, Travis."

"I know that. I meant home like…here, I guess. I rented an apartment downtown. Close enough for Mia to walk and…for us to walk."

"Us," she repeated, feeling the first true spark of hope light in her heart. He wasn't playing games this time. He loved her, and he wanted to stay.

"I'm sorry, Gena. About…everything, but I've smartened up and I want to spend the rest of my life with you."

She was sobbing again, but she threw her arms around him, and he had to act fast to keep them both from tumbling down the stairs.

He lifted her in his arms and carried her down to the living room, where he sat her in the rocking chair. He fumbled in his pocket, and Gena's throat seemed to swell up, until she could barely breathe.

He cleared his throat then knelt in front of her, and Gena started to tremble. "This might sound kind of stupid."

Gena wanted to reassure him it wouldn't, but she was unable speak. This couldn't really be happening to her. She had to be asleep, and any moment she would wake—alone—in her bed.

"I went to the jeweler, and I didn't…I didn't want to just trade one ring for another because it seemed…cheap. And I didn't see anything that was special enough for you."

He raised his hand with the fingers still clenched, hiding what lay in his palm. "I want to give you this, because I wish I had given it to you so many years ago."

He opened his hand, and Gena's heart melted. She ran her fingertip over the huge class ring, feeling the large ruby and the engraved football insignia, his initials, and the year they graduated. That was the year—just barely—that Mia had been born. It was strung on a gold chain.

"Will you marry me again, Gena Taylor?"

Her heart seemed to stop beating for a second, and she had trouble breathing. Tears streamed down her face as she said the hardest words she had ever had to say. "I…I c-can't."

He froze, and she watched the emotions play across his face—disbelief, confusion, a little bit of anger. "You can't? I thought–" he stood and backed away "—I thought you loved me."

"I do. I love you *so* much. That's why you've been able to tear my heart to shreds, and I…"

She tried to find the words to explain the fear that was seeping through her—the distrust. "You've jerked me around like a yo-yo, Travis, and I can't—won't—do it anymore."

He shoved his hands in his pockets, staring down at his feet. "I'm sorry, Gena. I just couldn't admit what I was feeling for you. I don't…I don't know what else I can say."

Gena felt as if her life's blood was pouring out onto the ground and she was helpless to stop it. "We haven't even been able to have a decent conversation for more than five minutes. We don't even know each other that well."

Suddenly he was kneeling at her feet again, looking earnestly up into her eyes. "Then we'll try. We'll take as much time as you need.

"And you're right—maybe we could know each other a little better. But I know I love you. I know that I want to spend the rest of my life with you. Let me prove it to you."

"I want to...I do love you, Travis. I'm just scared that—"

"Don't be. There is nobody else now. It's you and me and our daughter. I know in my heart that we will be happy."

He reached up and touched her cheek, and she turned her face, pressing against his hand. "I want to."

"Then marry me. We'll have the wedding when you're ready, but promise me now you'll be my wife."

When she looked down into his blue eyes, all her doubts fled. He loved her, and she loved him with a strength that took her breath away. It was a chance at happiness that she couldn't risk throwing away, no matter what the outcome may be.

"Yes," she whispered, savoring the sound of that one simple word. It sounded so right.

Travis's grin lit up his entire face. "You will?"

She launched herself at him from the rocker and they tumbled to the ground. "Yes!" she screamed, then kissed him.

Gena barely managed to stifle her laughter until he was out of earshot. "I hope he doesn't remember this in the morning."

"Speaking of morning, who's going to come over and help me unpack?"

Mia looked uncertainly at her mother. "Maybe...well, you guys probably want some time alone, huh?"

Travis ruffled her hair. "There will be plenty of time for that *after* the wedding—" he looked at Gena "—which will be when?"

"Soon," she whispered, soaking in the love shining in his eyes.

"Definitely," he growled, and kissed her again.

Epilogue

Gena paused at the top of the front staircase, her gaze sweeping over the formal parlor. Nobody had seen her yet and she basked in the warmth and love that filled her heart.

The Riverside Inn was at its best for Christmas Eve. The Yankee candles lit throughout the room and the festive tree in the corner filled her senses with the familiar and beloved scents of the season.

Twinkling lights framed the large bow window, and reflected on the white landscape beyond. The boughs of the trees outside were heavy with newly fallen snow, their tips bearing shimmering drops of ice which festively mirrored the large lights strung around the outside of the house. A fire blazed in the fireplace and from the dining room she could smell the bounty of home-baked apple pies and the turkey that had just come out of the oven, thanks to her mother.

Everybody she loved was in the room and she let her gaze fall on each of them in turn. Mia sat at the piano, softly playing Gena's favorite Christmas hymns. Her red dress and bow were accented by the poinsettias resting atop the piano.

Her parents sat on the loveseat, watching their granddaughter play and Gena said a silent prayer, thankful they had arrived in time. Their flight had been delayed—almost cancelled—because of the weather, but Travis had been able to get them at the airport about noon. The night would not have been the same without them.

Travis's mother sat in the wingback chair, also watching her granddaughter play. In the two months since Travis had proposed she had started warming up to the idea of their marriage, and she actually looked like she was enjoying herself. There hadn't been any more talk about corruption, at least.

Jill Delaney stood in front of the tree in a red dress that was identical to Mia's. Travis's father stood next to her, and it looked like they were managing a lively conversation. Gena smiled as she watched them. Any conversation that included Jill was lively.

Finally she looked at Travis. Her heart seemed to swell with so much love she wasn't sure how it managed to fit in her chest.

He looked nervous in his tuxedo, and he kept tugging at his waist, adjusting the red cummerbund. His face was slightly flushed and she smiled, thankful he was feeling the same emotions she was.

The thought had hit her the second she opened her eyes that morning and it still hadn't quite sunk in. *Today's the day I become Mrs. Travis Ryan. Again.*

But it would be different this time. Instead of getting the license and marrying immediately, they had decided to wait. The last two months had been full of the joy of learning to be a family, and now they were ready.

Tears stung her eyes and she blinked them away. Tomorrow morning she would wake up beside her husband, and together they would watch Mia's childish joy when she opened the pile of gifts bearing her name under the tree.

A real family, she thought with a contented sigh. She reached up by habit, her fingers running over the class ring around her neck.

Travis had dragged her to one jeweler after another, but she hadn't found a ring that could replace the one he had given her the night he returned from Boston. She would wear his class ring around her neck forever, and in a few minutes he would place on her finger the simple band with the Celtic design they had chosen. And she would do the same.

"Mrs. Travis Ryan," she whispered softly.

Travis pulled at the ridiculous band around his waist again, cursing it under his breath.

It was his own fault, though. Remembering their first wedding ceremony, in a dusty civic office, he had insisted on giving Gena the wedding she wanted. Thus, the tux and the uncomfortable cummerbund.

Jittery and anxious to begin, he made sure the Justice of the Peace was in his place, then smiled at their parents. His father would act as his best man, and Jill was the maid of honor. They were both where they needed to be, so all he could do was wait.

Mia caught his eye and smiled, never missing a note. He winked at her, thanking God for what had to be the thousandth time for giving him this daughter. The rush of emotion was almost too much to bear, so he cleared his throat and looked up at the stairs again.

Gena was there, looking down at him with so much love that his throat seemed to close up on him. She was radiant and no force on earth could have made him look away from her.

Her hand cradled the heavy ring that always rested a little below the hollow of her throat, framed by the sweetheart neckline of the exquisite ivory gown she wore. Her hair was swept up, revealing the graceful arch of her neck and the ruby earrings she had chosen to match the ring. In her free hand she held a bouquet of red roses and baby's breath.

The music changed, heralding the bride's arrival, so he knew the others had seen her, but still he couldn't drag his gaze away from hers. Her hazel eyes never left his as she walked slowly down the stairs and he stretched out his hand.

She took it and a tremor shook his body. *What have I ever done to deserve this woman?*

"I love you," he whispered as the Justice of the Peace began to speak.

They repeated their vows and Travis felt a sense of completeness he had never thought possible. Each word he said echoed through his heart, etching itself onto his very soul. He would love her forever. He would forsake all others and he would cherish her for as long as he lived.

Finally they were man and wife, and as he leaned forward to kiss her, she smiled up at him. *That smile*—the one he had yearned for, for so many years. And this one was just for him.

Shannon Stacey

Shannon Stacey married her Prince Charming in 1993, and is the proud mother of a future Nobel Prize for Science-winning bookworm and an adrenaline junkie with a flair for drama. She lives in New England, where her two favorite activities are trying to stay warm and writing stories of happily ever after.

You can contact Shannon through her website: www.shannonstacey.com

Now available in print!

Stud Finders Incorporated
By Alexis Fleming
1-59998-042-8

Wanted -- An Orgasm... and the chance to fulfill all her sexual fantasies.

Madison believes she's frigid. Her ex told her so and maybe it's true, because there's one thing she's never experienced. An orgasm! Now she wants it all. So when her mother rings Stud Finders Incorporated and hires a stud for her to practice on, why look a gift horse in the mouth?

Jake's ex-lover said he was boring, both in bed and out. So when sexy Madison asks him to teach her to have an orgasm, he jumps at the chance to prove his manhood. Even if it means hiding the fact that the purpose of Stud Finders Incorporated is to find the studs behind the wallboards of a building so the owner can safely hang his paintings.

Warning: This book contains hot, explicit sex between two people explained in graphic language.

Now available in print!

Loup Garou
By Mandy M. Roth
1-59998-043-6

Lindsay Willows craves a simple life. One where she can make a difference without drawing too much attention to herself. As the daughter of both a vampire and a fay, the cards were already stacked against her. Finding out she's the supposed mate of a dark fay prince doesn't help matters. Especially when there are those who will stop at nothing to prevent her from mating with a prince she's never even met.

When Exavier Kedmen, the incredibly sexy front man for a world-famous band, shows up wanting her to go back to a field she left three years ago, she can't explain the strong feelings that surface for a man she barely knows. Lindsay finds herself confronting demons from her past, coming to terms with the ones in the present and finally looking forward to a future with the man she was created for. And she discovers evil doesn't care who it hurts to obtain its goals but even the evilest of things fear something, or in the case of Exavier, someone.

Warning: This book contains hot, explicit sex and violence explained with contemporary, graphic language.

Samhain Publishing, Ltd.

It's all about the story...

Action/Adventure
Fantasy
Historical
Horror
Mainstream
Mystery/Suspense
Non-Fiction
Paranormal
Red Hots!
Romance
Science Fiction
Western
Young Adult

http://www.samhainpublishing.com

Printed in the United States
66478LVS00005B/163-276

9 781599 980447